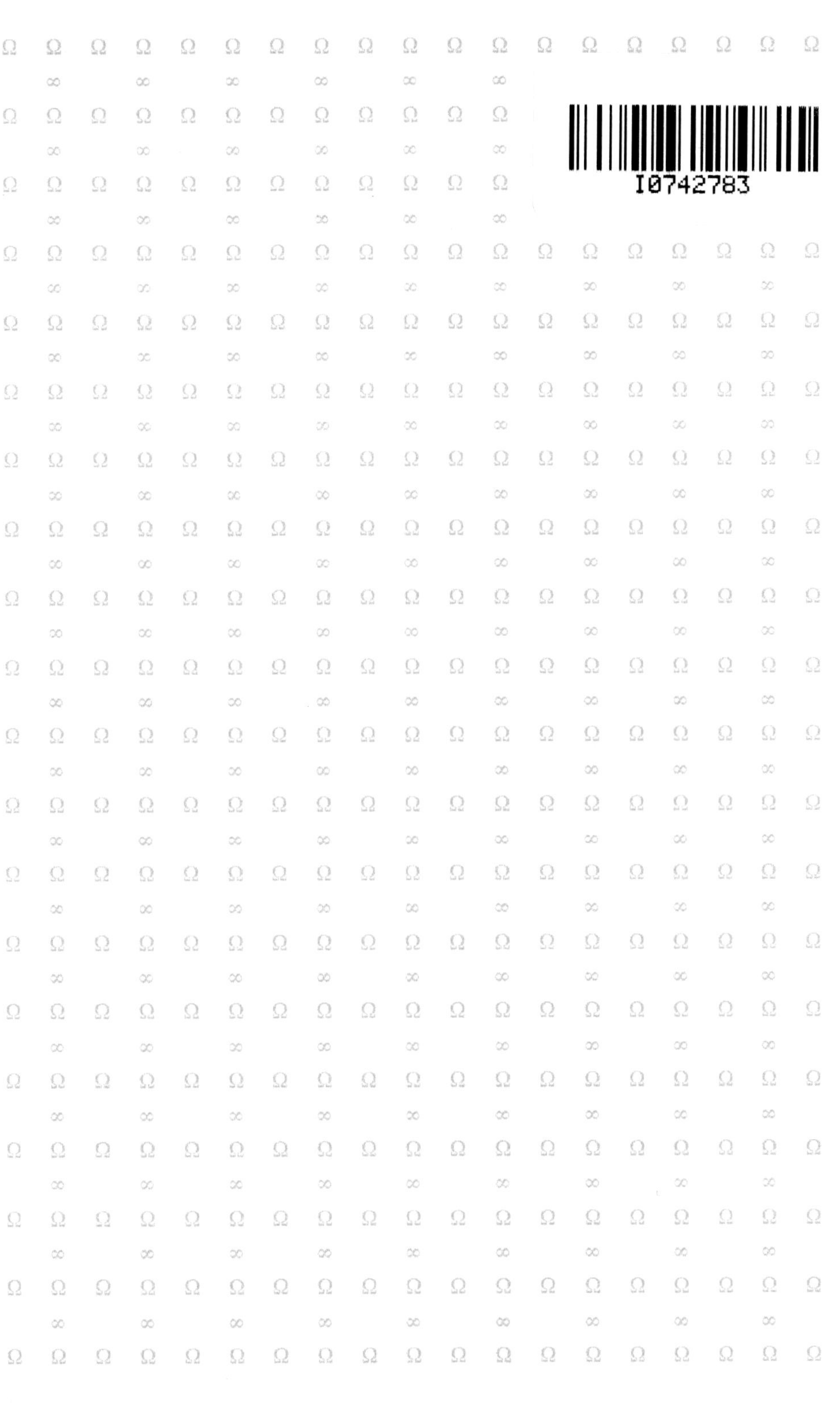

I0742783

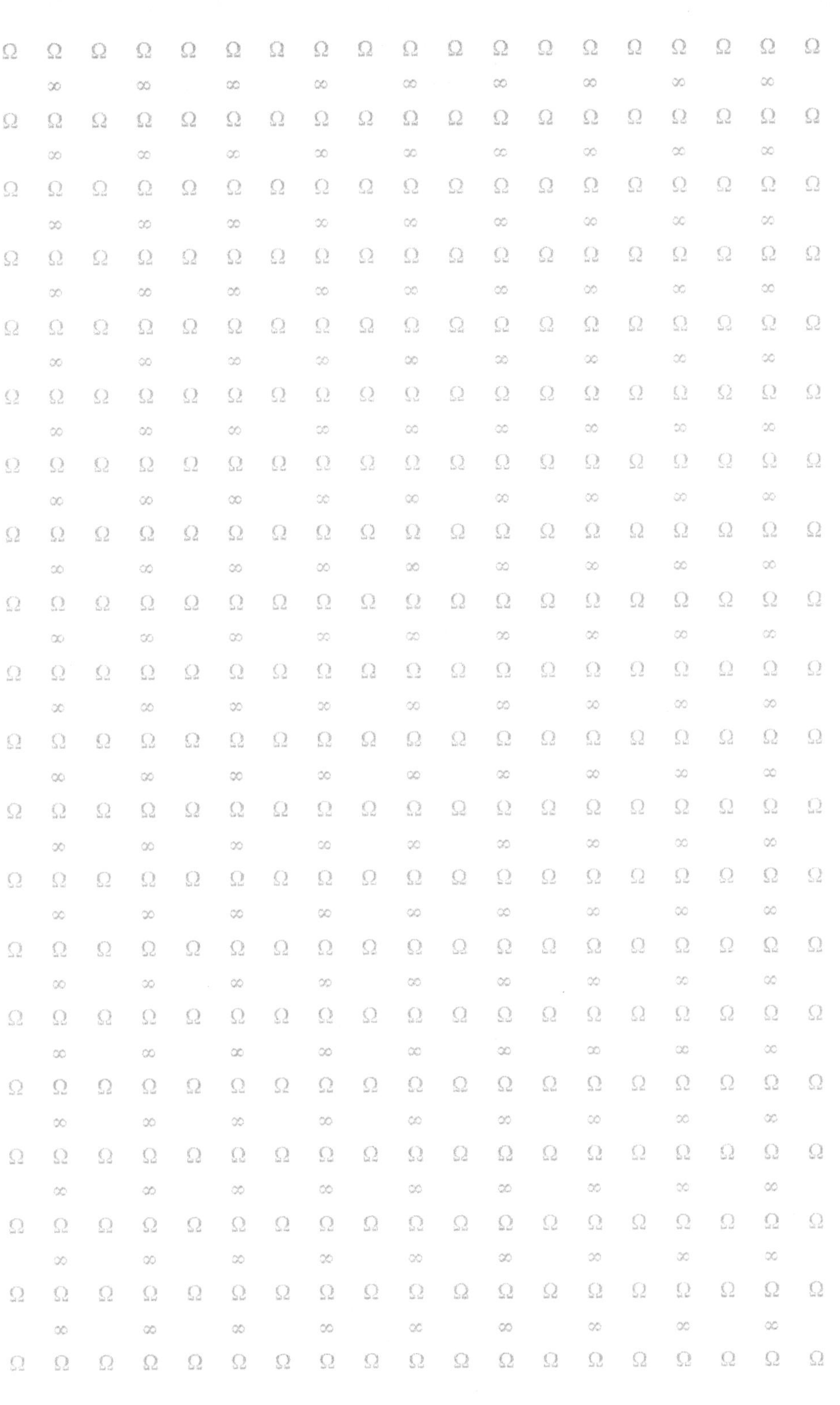

# Hidden Valley
## A love story

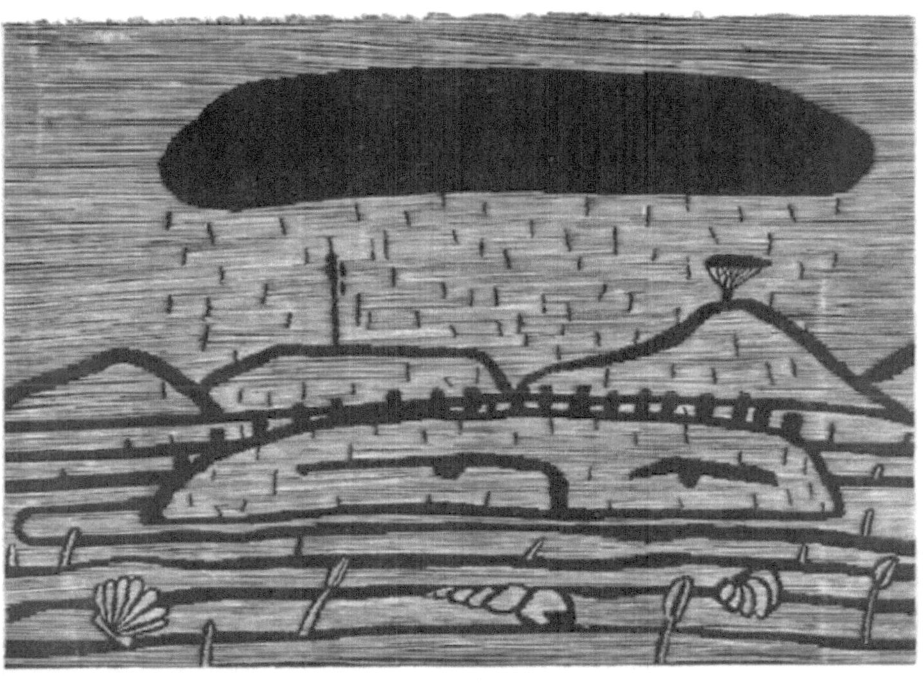

# Hidden Valley
## A *love story*

**David L. Hume**

**in case of emergency press**
*https://icoe.com.au*
Travancore, Victoria
Australia

Published by **in case of emergency press** 2022



ISBN 978-0-6453751-7-6

Cover and Title Page art:
Michael Schlitz © 2014

*To the water's edge
we flock
in search of safe harbour,
like thousands before.
Strangers unknown, unwanted,
dislocated, displaced.
First world refugees.*

# Table of contents

## Acknowledgement

I would like to acknowledge the spirit that rises
from the land to inhabit all that rests upon it and
the real people who might glimpse of a fragment
of themselves in the imagined characters that
make this story possible.

**David L. Hume**

# Dedication

For Sandra, my fellow adventurer.

# Hidden Valley

*A love story*

# Chapter 1

## Hidden Valley

Hidden Valley is a place of fortune and misfortune, depending on how you look at it. It is a place founded by shipwreck. Established by the flotsam and jetsam washed ashore from foundered vessels, The Argo, most likely The King George III, quite possibly The Louisa and probably The Enchantress.

The lives said to be lost were those of unfortunates transported to these shores.

Other unfortunates, who should not, but often are forgotten, or are included as a kind of subtitle for political correctness, are of course the indigenous folk and culture dispossessed, slaughtered in a war of invasion or "integrated" by this foam of whiteness that surfed the world and washed upon these and other grounds of hunt and gather and knowing engagement.

The Valley, as the locals call it, has the rare, if not unique, distinction of being without a war memorial. No obelisk of inscribed sandstone, slow to warm, forever leaching, littering junctions, roundabouts, or set central in a community park. Not in the so called Great or subsequent, Less Great second did any settlement of Hidden Valley commit or lose men. As a result, ANZAC Day, that often contentious display of now ancient courage and blind obedience, almost lost to living memory, passes by unnoticed.

It wasn't until almost a century past settlement, between the two wars, that the folk of Hidden Valley came to know their place, then themselves and even this came as the result of misfortune.

Unable to gather cultural and artistic insights from Europe and Mother England, when, like the rest of the country, the

Valley was in dire economic straits, soup kitchens, starving families, rabbit trappers going bust, during the depression of the nineteen thirties, folk turned inward to discover themselves, finally appreciating the majestic landscape under their collective snouts. The community discovered its own vernacular, way of seeing, writing and being, too. One such place to come to the attention of the newly inward looking was Hidden Valley and then the Lost West, or Empty Corner, as blinkered fools came to call it, that in so many ways nourished Hidden Valley.

Until then Hidden Valley had remained largely untouched, or at least somewhat insulated, at arm's length from war, plague, famine and other maladies of the world at large and, indeed, benefited from the result of some.

For example, without the advances in transportation brought by the horrors of the Great War, the motor car would likely not have been as common as it was during the depression and places like the Lost West, Tarn Field, The Broken Heart Range and Lost Lake would not have been within reach for weekend expeditions from the metropolis of Sallyman Cove.

Prior to the rise of the motor vehicle, the high mountain ridge to the north of Hidden Valley had only been passable during a small summer window and then only by brave souls who ignored tales of fierce tigers and demented trolls with dreadlocked heads of fiery red, their ashen skin draped in grey and snowy hair, their mating call trumpeted from toothless gobs sounding a lot like an elongated "Hey noddy-noddeeeee" yodel. One is pure myth, designed to deter civilized city folk from venturing into primeval nature and the root of racist fear in difference. The other is rarely seen but romantically propagated.

Such, indeed, are the wheels of misfortune that a second wave of settlers filtered into Hidden Valley. Folk that first came by charabanc to walk the hills of the Lost West and marvel at the forests, returned to find solace from a world going mad for the second time in a lifetime. They brought with them ideas formerly unknown to the Bergers, Reeves, Graylarches, Penwrights, Frints and McThis and McThats from half the highland clans of Scotland. To name the most present and remembered of those who crawled from the wreckage of ships. Most now remembered as names of minor streets, creeks, hills and marshes.

The new folk carried with them belief systems the folk of the wrecks could barely pronounce, mostly because they had no patience for words with more than four syllables, or understood what an "ology" or an "ism" was. These folk of complex tongues built log cabins and adobe huts in narrow valleys, cleared forests they first marvelled at and wrote poetically of, and subsisted on a ration of flour, sugar and tea and what could be caught, trapped, hunted and occasionally grown. Of forage they were shy, good meat being easier to identify than poisonous plants.

It was some forty years on that the next disturbances to the shipwrecked came. Arriving from foreign shores with different tongues and less superstition they gravitated again to the hills and mountains, and saw fortune and opportunity in the misfortunes of changing agricultural markets and the sale and subdivision of farms expected to be inherited. Again they sought peace and solace from a world spiralling out of control, and to find a new way, one less reliant on treading other folk into the mud.

By now Hidden Valley, like Garden Island, or Meat and Potato Bay was not really hidden, more forgotten to all but odd folk that fell for the romantic landscape and the idea of living at the end of the earth. A bit like Norway.

Unless it received a massive tourist promotion or a prize for something like its outstanding landscape, clean air, quality food, or being maniacally happy, most people forgot about it and left the few sparsely flung folk who lived there to get on as they chose.

It gained the name Hidden, because to get into it you had to climb a winding road over a high mountain that in winter was snowbound and challenged strangers at what the locals called The Cold Shoulder, replete with the aforementioned trolls and tigers and more recently dismembering accidents, that preceded most plans to set out. Or you had to sail along a stunning coastline, so mesmerizingly gorgeous it was called The Cote de Distraction by the early French explorers, due to the number of ships that foundered upon its hidden reefs and rocky shores because everyone, including those that were supposed to be at the helm, were so gobsmacked at its extreme beauty, that like Homer's sailors they were lured to disaster.

Today yachts and leisure craft continue to fall foul of its bars and reefs. Only advances in navigation aids has made it possible for some vessels to return from what has synaesthesitically been renamed the Siren Coast for the ease of the Anglophone.

❀

Local legend has it that the first settlers to the region, founders of the town of Shipwreck, were as a result of The Argo and those later doomed ships.

Two dozen wretched folk, it is said, washed ashore, survivors from an illicit hijacking out in Sallyman Cove by a gang of convicts. Some descendants walk the streets now while, over the years, many more have succumbed to the dazzle of Sallyman Cove and beyond.

The raft, or wreckage, from which the two dozen stepped ashore, or more likely fell into the waist high black, sucking, estuarine mud, and dragged their way to terra firma, has, like much historical narrative in these parts, shifted in form and content.

It is thought by some that the deep goop, that stretches far up into the town of Shipwreck and as far south as Survivors Bay, has preserved the raft in its entirety, along with some of the bodies that had no strength to drag themselves ashore. Others are more convinced, having studied the flow of tide and current with approximated models of smashed and lashed timber, that it would have been washed back out to sea and broken up.

The shape of the salvation vessel, however, has over time and following numerous renderings in gouache, watercolour, acrylic and oils, together with plasticine, clay, papier-mâché, balsa and most ambitiously of all a life-size sculpture of twisted and welded scrap metal, that now rests at the junction of the high street and esplanade, come to look a lot like Theodore Gericault's notorious painting *The Raft of the Medusa*. Again history is plastic and has a habit of aggrandizement, often stoked by survivors and their descendants.

All we can, reasonably, be sure of is the Argo disappeared from Sallyman Cove in 1814 and was never seen again. The rest is a matter of conjecture for historians to debate and the citizens of Shipwreck to bicker about, as some families have been doing for the last two centuries.

The Valley runs north-south down to the bay, meaning the sharp north end, until it gains some altitude, gets stinking hot in the summer, while the low south lands are ventilated by a cooling sea breeze. However the lowlands are also fog bound in the winter, while the highlands benefit from crisp, health-giving air above the fog line. Both have their advantages, but the coastal areas are, as with most of this hollow country, the most populated parts and the higher up and more inland you travel the more insecure it gets.

You see people, even total strangers, gather together for security in the face of the unknown, like the ancient tribes that lived here before the raft.

However, unlike tribes the world over, and their discreet villages, most people today don't know when to start over and set up another village. So they just keep tacking bits on, like dozens of urchin children clinging to mother's hems, and soon the whole thing becomes harder and harder to manage and mother's frock falls away.

Shipwreck is getting that way. But this has nothing to do with this story, as most folk who came to live in Hidden Valley in the days immediately following the raft were stubbornly independent buggers, hoping to find their own way and unconsciously establish their own tribe with its own customs and odd little ways.

Where once the bush, of tall Stringy Bark and sedgy grasses stretched almost to the coast, before giving way to She Oaks and more tough coastal sedge, now the grass is soft and manicured and the trees sawn into timber, much of it used in the old vertical board places of four square rooms and a later built in veranda for the modern convenience of an inside toilet and bathroom.

These houses rise densely along the bay, snaking around the esplanade, interrupted briefly by a few later built weatherboards, and line the lower reaches of the main road a little less densely. The abodes thin to farms as they rise to the north and leave the town of Shipwreck.

Having been built in the time of horses and carts, before the period of six cylinders and bitumen, most are close, sometimes too close, to the main road, their perpendicularity dislodged by the rumble of trucks.

At the western end of the Esplanade, remnant forests still come close, where the land curves round into a wooded point, and low cliffs descend like a giant staircase into the sea. The leeward side is home to nesting seabirds, the occasional basking seal and that other rare species in these parts, young lovers, huddled in rock shelters.

Here the town of Shipwreck begins and ends in a jaunty row of a dozen vertical board shacks, rough sawn, now silver muted, one inch thick timber boards, a more narrow one inch square strip over the join. Some have been daubed with paint of a mock Aegean sort of blue and white and decorated with lobster pots and old cork life rings. Under the persistent slate of southern skies they rarely shine as desired. Most folks are happy with the natural bleaching that in many ways renders them an architectural and chromatic link between sea and forest.

There were once more, as there were once wattle and daub shacks and before that bark shelters, where these grey survivors stand. These modest low rise cottages were later punctuated by double storey sheds in the same style, thus reinforcing the perception of vertical board as industrial or at least utilitarian. The old fruit packing and dehydrating sheds with vented pitch and sentinel rows of peeling, coring, slicing and dicing machines, like science fiction guards, seem to mark the end of waterfront industry and the advent of horizontal domesticity and services with a strip of narrow fronted weatherboard cottages, deeper and darker than they are wide and sunny, despite the run of lines dragging the eye along the street.

The easy row of a dozen, almost identical and neatly kept, reputedly federation houses, is broken by the odd mansion style, boasting steep pitched roofs and abrupt dormer windows and a couple of jarring grossly renovated cottages clad in corrugated roofing iron on the horizontal, to affect the illusion of weatherboards and maintain the appearance of domesticity, without the need to paint every two or three years. Up the other end of the bay the tin stands in the vertical, its salt sprayed patina showing that even iron cannot deny age and nature.

Some of the old farmhouses on the outskirts that stretch up the valley, retain their original land holding, but most exist as small, inconvenient cut outs with tiny allotments, surrounded by bigger farms, watched over by more modern homes of mostly brick, that are easier to warm and cool and not as susceptible to the rumble of trucks along the main road.

❋

To the southwest, the seemingly never ending mountain range stretches beyond the eye, and heavy cumulus clouds moodily drift and sometimes roar with the cry of wronged banshees. Rising to high button grass planes and stunted Snow

Gums, then dropping, seemingly without warning, into precipitous gorges of bone crushing rivers, it is scarp to test the nerve and tendons of most. In winter the peaks glisten with snow and intensify the light on the windward, often unseen face of Hidden Valley. This is a landscape to inspire latter day Romantic painters, with its mists and peaks of wonder and Hasselblad-wielding photographers in its deep ravines.

It does not benefit from the trapped sun, or long ripening summers of the lowlands. Day comes late to many of these peaks and even later to the southern facing clefts. As a result, the pattern of settlement on this edge of the wilderness, bent by biting westerlies, has been erratic with some ingress along narrow rivers, cliff tops and extending to the remote rough grazing pastures of Hidden Valley farms that reach westward like mischievous fingers dipping into the unknown. Fixed dwellings were limited to clusters of timber getters' shacks from the nineteenth century and the occasional hamlet where travellers took rest in rustic unlicensed ale houses and hardy pioneers sought to eke out a living from hard won and desperately marginal farms and orchards.

One such cluster is Lonelyvale. Once a timber getters' camp, high in the hills then expanded through land grants of substantial size, and more recently a few outlying homesteads. Its once vibrant infrastructure now a ghost, visible only in its surviving buildings abutting directly to the road and overgrown forest tramways that once careered with logs plundered from the deep forest.

Here, as in The Glen, just over the hill, Bloodbury, or nearby Sourtree, the frost and snow settle hard in winter and have been known to rest for weeks.

While vacant of centre, Lonelyvale is not without a community, albeit scattered among the hills, single folk enjoying close to a hermit existence, couples setting out on their own path, and extended family encampments of three generations or more founded on trauma and desolation. Some more recent properties appear as country lodges, like warts against the backdrop of tall gums, disconnected by acres of prim and always trimmed lawns and pet grazed paddocks populated with exotic sheep, rare breed cattle, and or tricoloured alpacas.

Doc Dory lives in one such property. There are many Docs in the Valley, but not many that know much about illness and injury like Doc Dory. A woman of translucent skin and falling blubber, she bought her place twelve years ago, following the passing of her partner and semi retirement, 70 odd acres of bush and pasture, almost one for each of her years.

Despite there being some sort of heritage covenant on the property, she burnt down the original house, a rotten timber homestead, and built a brand new brick and tile mansion, complete with one entire paddock of solar panels and the latest off grid technology. Some folk suggested she burnt down the original place for the insurance but most can see the insurance would not have built the five bedroom, four bathroom, three garages and stables she replaced it with.

Her nearest neighbours, about ten kilometres up the valley, as the raven flies, are the Coboldis. Theirs is not brick and tile, but pink fibro, with a collection of iron clad sheds, one of which harbours a clanking old generator for when the power goes out, as it often does. Neither do the Coboldis have stables. They did have a garage, but Ma and Pa Coboldi, who bought the property in the time of fibro, live in that now, while Shanty, their granddaughter, raises a brood of the next generation of Coboldis in the main house with her partner Dazza. Shanty's Mum Carly, formerly known as Skyblue and before that her real name Cheryl, lives with Trev, whose real and only name is Trevor, in a hole in the ground up the hill a bit, beside a creek from which they only ever venture as far as the main house.

Carly used to live with Stevo, Trev's mate, but one night they were sitting around a campfire and looked at the stars and saw a whole line of lights traversing the sky. Round and round, circling them. Trev started talking conspiracy theories and aliens and the end of the world and Skyblue, as she was then, was besotted, so Stevo left and moved in with Janey, Trev's sister, who is quite ordinary and works part time at the school and part time at the local shop. Stevo is also quite ordinary and works a couple of bays down at a secretive seaweed farm, where they are developing a super food to feed the world from a rare kelp.

Stevo and Trev don't talk anymore, mostly because Trev doesn't go out. He hasn't been seen out of home for five years, while Carly has been seen twice during that period. Instead they grow beans and salt meat and store it in their bunker that they dug over the last 10 years.

Shane, Shanty's brother, lives in a caravan next to the garage every now and then, when he's not working in the mines. There are at least fifteen other Coboldi households littered about the Valley in various villages and locales.

A number of paddocks surround the Coboldi compound. In the middle of each are at least three dead vans or station wagons, home to a herd of pigs that are shuffled between paddocks when the ploughing is done and reduced in number at the end of every summer. The Coboldis, in many ways, represent more properties in the Valley than Doc Dory's but people don't talk about them much.

As you descend down the Valley, toward Shipwreck, the shape of the landholdings changes from wide and broad to narrow ribbons of land, surveyed from road's edge up and over hills that give way to less travelled tracks. Some properties widen as they rise to the hills but many maintain parallel boundaries, in spite of natural geographical markers.

In contrast the northern hills, at the foot of the dominating range, appear inviting. More rolling pastures, punctuated by the odd wooded rise, dotted with idyllic towns and hamlets. They dip from gently curved hilltop, gradually down to the fertile valley floor. Almost as settled and benign as the rolling downs of England, they have invited settlement from the days of those first two dozen.

Easy slopes to ascend, with their advantageous outlooks, they now offer a vista of orchards and paddocks, and early settlers were quick to seize and build upon them. With the wealth of harvests generated from properties on this side of the valley, the main road was developed in their service, reaching from the bay up to the sharp end of the valley, where the trees grow thicker and the people more sparse, before ascending its way through more remote settlements, and lastly zigzagging to the dreaded range of trolls and tigers.

There are a few surviving homesteads along the lower section of the road.

Very few, however, are as productive as they once were, while some exist in name only, allocated to the entry road into five acre subdivisions that provide a soundscape of ride on mowers most weekends and the screech of tightly strung mini trail bikes when the grandchildren visit to buzz around paddocks, that are otherwise grazed by beasts to be ridden or petted.

The Whistlebrows live in the biggest surviving property. They inherited an almond and hazel nut orchard when they bought it and keep a herd of sixty head of Highland Cattle, for petting only. Both Whistlebrows live in town during the week, where they teach something as unproductive as their paddocks, to students who just want to create pretty pictures and cute cuddly things, or think a turd in a bucket is art. They engage local folk and holiday makers to harvest the nuts from their trees and turn the harvest into *milk*, which they then sell online at a premium.

The local folk look forward to the harvest, for which they carry away baskets of nuts like grateful squirrels and take high tea in the grounds, with the occasional tour into the big house, which is a classic old homestead, kept very neat inside and out and serves as a reminder to the locals of how cold and draughty the old houses are and the extraordinary amount of wood and electricity it takes to warm them.

Either side of the Whistlebrows is a weekend alpaca park and a mini goat paddock. That's a full size paddock with goats the size of beagles.

✺

Between the fertile slopes and the steep scarp, leading down to the beach is a small, old style high street, lined with shops on one side and a primary school with three teachers and two mixed class grades catering to thirty odd pupils, a nursing centre and brick town hall on the other. The shops include Reeves the butcher, smoking its own bacon, the aroma of which pervades the entire village twice a week, much to the annoyance of some recently settled folk, the post office and newsagent, a fast food come pizza and fish and chip shop, a general store with an identity crisis, struggling between supermarket and hardware, and an empty bank. Like bookends the street is punctuated north and south by two pubs. Both churches, on the high ground behind the school, burnt down under mysterious circumstances about thirty years ago and the people of Shipwreck voted not to rebuild them as they had other things to do. Besides the only folk that spoke of God when they weren't cursing lived up in the hills and hardly ever came to town.

Known as Ancy's, the general store carries a name descended from the first two dozen raftees, beneath the franchise brand. Clancy Berger is a short squat man, like an over inflated balloon with a bespectacled face drawn on, that walks in tight shoes that pinch his corns. He is the sort of bloke that reckons he runs the town, while most folk in the Valley reckon he bullies his wife at best. His claim to owning Shipwreck is based on Bart Berger the forger being the first off the raft, a second or two before Sleepy Reeves the sheep stealer.

Both Clancy and Simo Reeves run thriving businesses that provide the basics for the people of the Valley, like sausages and bacon, nails and toilet paper. Their families have intermarried a number of times over the last hundred and fifty years.

Clancy is also a member of, or has been a member of, every committee that exists in the town of Shipwreck, with the exception of the Country Women's Association. While his most ambitious power grab has been thwarted at every turn, failing to achieve a seat on the local council five times, and currently on his sixth attempt. It seems that while the shop is a success with a friendly welcome and much of what he stocks necessary, his reputation does not translate into a popular vote.

The waterfront is home, almost exclusively, to what Clancy and others refer to as *Blowins*, with varying degrees of welcome and disdain. Mostly superannuated mainlanders who have discovered the pleasures of not so Hidden Valley, most likely as a result of one of those prizes it won for its pristine beauty, fresh air, relaxed lifestyle, or smiling a lot like manic inmates.

They blow in and blow out according to the season, scurrying off in the depths of winter to family in sunnier parts, in cities where they spent their productive years as public servants, and accountants—taxes collected and taxes avoided—scientists, engineers, small business operators, and teachers, oh oodles of teachers, especially music and art teachers. All attracted by the prospect of buying a little bit of heritage on the waterfront with a view of the bay, or at least with water glimpses while perched on the toilet.

Some are content to take in the views on a daily basis, admiring the ocean, their sparkly little boats bobbing up and down in the bay, and contributing to local volunteer groups to engender themselves into the community.

Others, less adept at doing nothing, gardening, learning piano, banjo or fiddle, watercolour painting, or writing memoirs, or simply unable to unshackle from a working life, suffering from an aching void of identity, fill their time by morphing into yoga teachers, Reiki or Shiatsu practitioners, lifestyle coaches, relationship councillors, mindset advisors and so on, or take it in turns to open and close cafes. Usually the same cafe with a different name.

❁

Along the esplanade and reaching into the soft low hills behind, where ancient forests are long past, and that planted within living memory, evident now only in warty unkempt fruit trees, limbs weak with rot, compound fractures of arched limbs, torn beneath the groan of unwanted fruit, is the stubble of past wealth.

Such remnants exist around the edges of fields where machinery cannot reach, in hard to get at patches of the Valley, along rutted roads, shadowy clefts, on once prime flat land, now boggy delta swamps, patrolled by swans in deep silhouette and dive bombing bandit plovers.

It was quickly recognised that the climate suited the fruit of the old country and the second generation, spawned of the raft folk, imported a vast range of berry bushes and vines, stone fruit, apples and pears. Their aim to extend the eating of fresh fruit as long as possible, for most had the wisdom of eating fresh fruit passed down to them by their wistful parents, who remembered the health-giving properties imparted by their mothers, as well as the sweetness of that sun warmed first pluck of home they would never see again.

Within a few more generations, the outside world poked its paternal nose over the cold shoulder and around the point and the great variety, the almost constant supply of fresh fruit and berries was depleted in the name of integration and market forces. However the fickle fashion for fruit, sweet, tart, large, lunchbox size, red, green and golden, has ever since made the orchardist life a constant challenge.

One or two old farms have, mostly by accident, preserved a few of the old fruit trees and vines. Like fashion in anything if you wait long enough it comes back around. Now they call them heritage or heirloom varieties. The folk of the Valley call them old time berries or by the name of the landowner that prunes, thins, and protects them from predatory blackbirds and parrots and sells them in roadside stalls and once a year at the monthly market.

The new folk, the flotsam that has washed into the old fisherman shacks, and the few commercial outlets that set up in the early days, butchers, bakers, seamstresses, cobblers, blacksmiths and the like, often seek specimen trees and vines to set in a heritage corner of the garden, and lend a sense of belonging and provide their grandchildren with a story to tell when they return to school after summer holidays at Grannie's cottage by the sea, like it's an ancestral home. History and heritage, like stock and scions, can be quickly spliced but take more than graduation from toddler to puberty to form that tough gnarled join that is perhaps, at best, set only for the next generation climb upon.

✸

In the falling hills, with their lush and inviting pastures rolling in and out of gentle folds, the grass now grows long and is cut for hay at the end of each year and into the first weeks of the next. It's a task that interferes with the traditional festive season of relaxation and feasting, so is contracted out now by weekend farmers to the remaining true farmers further from the water's edge. The people of the land who know how to maintain machinery, read the weather and don't let pagan festivals get in the way of what needs doing.

And make some money to put aside for a rainy day, of which there seem to be more and more recently.

There is drinking money also to made by the young and strong of back, good money for a day's sweat lifting bales, often kids and young adults from the mountains, farms and villages, from families that once owned the land they now step on for less than a week a year. They stack heavy bales, some ready to burst if not lifted right, just high enough and keyed together so they can be driven back to the farm and unloaded into the barn their grandfather built when their fathers were their age.

A number of teenagers get their first driving experience manoeuvring tractors, towing house high trailers of hay, across bumpy fields. Under threat of reloading by themselves if they tip it, the concentration on their faces, the scanning for errant rocks and awareness of contours is writ on their pudgy cap shaded faces, like a cross between fear and the zoned in focus reserved usually for the footy field.

Once shorn of hay, the pet alpacas, mini goats, heritage breed sheep and misplaced cattle can be rotated onto the stubble and the owner's landscape painting restored to its gentrified serenity.

❀

It is unknown what would have become of the old farms and shacks and shops on the waterfront, protected by a narrow road from an unpredictable sea, just five meters below, their original use long past, before the flotsam arrived on a king tide of urban refugees, seeking a climate more acceptable to their age and condition. Some saw their retirement watching the waves erode the beach as they counted down their modest savings and measured the subsidence and rotting vertical or weather boards against their own expected due by dates. Others, often neighbours, would gut the former shops, leaving only the facade, pack the cavities with wads of insulation and line the walls with neutral tone plasterboard, lit from now recessed blue lights, an ensuite in every bedroom, then hang a bed and breakfast sign from the gantry that once weighed carcasses or sacks of flour, before they entered the shop.

The Bones run the six bedroom place three up from the corner with the main road. Wreck House they called it, with a humorous eye to the state of the place when they moved in. They'd washed up from a nondescript town deep inland: she retired from teaching at the local infants' school, where she'd been since graduation from teachers' college, and he a tradie at the nearby mine.

He'd not seen the sea in all of his 62 years. All he knew of it was from movies and stories she told of her time at college when she'd fallen in love with the ocean instead, of like other girls her age, other students.

Gus and June had met at high school and it turned out to be the one and only romance either wanted or needed. While she was learning to teach and swimming in the waves, he was learning to maintain things with wheels bigger than two storey houses. When she returned home, they married, had 0.7 more children than the average at the time: two girls and a boy, one dog and one cat and bought the house two streets along from his mum and dad, with a back yard that backed onto her mum and dad. Small inland towns tend to grow tight knit families that can only be escaped on death.

So it was with the Bones. The mine and dust had brought a premature end to three parents, while June's mother had given her last ounce of energy fighting for compensation, which she won posthumously.

The Bones, free from children themselves by then, having encouraged each to explore the world and follow their dreams before they got snagged in the town of dust and groaning machinery, took the opportunity to get out. For June it was to live a dream spawned in her youth. For Gus it was to realise the dreams engendered by the woman he lovingly called his little mermaid.

Almost all of the recent flotsam came to know the Bones, staying in the B&B for weeks or more as they waited eagerly for rewiring, plumbing, of some other necessary renovation to be carried out on their new home.

Next to Wreck House are the Furphy's. They came to Shipwreck five years back and did up one of the old weatherboard places. At first it wasn't known how they came across the property that had formerly been occupied by Mrs O'Donnel, once of the Raft Public House. There had been no real estate signs, no auction. It had rested empty, except for the ghost of Bridget O'Donnel. Then one day the Furphy's arrived, stopped with the Bones for three months while they cemented their standing in the community by bussing in every tradesperson and all the materials to renovate a similar falling down place. In three months the front facade was about all that remained. The interior completely gutted, rewired and relined with glorious plasterboard. The driveway, once thin cracked concrete was relayed and quickly gave way to an automatic garage door, that matched the shutters on every window.

Nigel Furphy kept working, even though in theory he'd retired. He suffered from fear of an idle brain and such had been his dedication to his profession for all his working life he'd lost the ability to think about anything else. The fact that he had two former wives and two teenagers to support might also have driven him. He also suffered from fear of an idle body, so the spare time he did grant himself was spent working on his yacht in the bay, which he could keep an eye on over a glass of Pinot from the front veranda. The third Mrs Furphy, Tonyaporn, formerly of Pataya, Thailand, seemed to be happy keeping house and Mr Furphy tidy.

❀

The last house in the row belonged to the Blanks, originally the Blancos, but it was changed many years ago in order to fit in, because Australians like to Anglicise anything foreign. Noreen and Dinghy Blank had been in the place ten years and loved their little old heritage cottage, with its slight lean toward the Furphys. It too was in need of a touch of TLC but Noreen and Dinghy didn't have a lot of money to chuck at it. They'd calculated that it would probably fall down when they did and until then would do just fine.

Dinghy was 70, overweight, his diabetes wasn't getting any better and no matter how he tried and how much Noreen nagged, in a loving way, he liked a beer and a smoke and could be spotted often on the front porch enjoying both, or in the driveway, under the tatty old carport, working on one of his dinghies. Noreen on the other hand didn't smoke and only drank a couple of glasses of Lambrusco on Sundays. But she knew her mother and grandmother both died at 86, so figured she had her expiry date.

Dinghy had four little boats, one timber planked, on which Noreen reckons he lavished more time and money than he did on her, one plywood, one fibreglass, that lived in the backyard and the grandkids used as a cubby house and an aluminium runabout or tinny, tied to a log across the road on the beach, like many of the other folk along the esplanade had. The only concession the Blanks made to the increasing gentrification was to paint the facade, which together with the well-kept wooden dinghies in the carport, gave the place a modicum of respectable tweeness. At least until Dinghy squeezed the rusty old troop carrier in the drive, which never quite fitted and always poked its nose onto the pavement, much to the disdain of Nigel Furphy.

Next to them on the corner was Raft Park, where the monthly markets are held. Dinghy is quite happy with the monthly disturbance next door and makes the most of the passing crowd by setting up shop in the driveway. You know, like a roadside vegie or plant stall. What Dinghy sells though he collects from the bay and nearby coves in his tinny, which he regards as his ute.

Unlike other folk with little boats, who return from journeys out to the bay with buckets and bins of fish, sometimes enough for the freezer and friends and even friend's freezers, Dinghy loads his boat with driftwood and other detritus washed up. Once dry and following a little brushing up and sometimes sanding to smooth off some edges, in order to imitate the work of sand and sea, he sets them out on the driveway with a price tag, ranging from $10 to $50, depending on size and how much each piece suggest the form of a person or some animal. If Dinghy sets out a dozen pieces, he rarely brings half a dozen in. In fact, one time a new fellow in town a couple of doors down bought the whole lot and the next day set about erecting a complete front fence, just to give his place that Shipwreck aesthetic.

There is indeed a reasonable market for crappy old bits of wood, and most that buy think they might be getting a piece of the original raft to decorate their bayside cottage or hobby farm. Dinghy isn't the sort of fellow to destroy people's dreams and delusions, especially when it might impact on his drinking and smoking budget.

❦

The pub across the road from the park is run by two bachelor cousins, Alex and Alistair McDonald, known as Big Al and Wee Al, born out of two brothers Alex and Alistair McDonald and their union with two sisters, Mary ard May McDonald nee McDougall. They'd thought about hyphenating their names, but then heard somewhere of an athlete named Mackeleemakombo and the last thing the sisters wanted was a suspicion of Africanness.

In their later years they'd taken up residence in the fireplace nook at the end of the main bar most days and really ran the pub, simply by their presence, as much as their sons. They could hardly be seen from the seclusion of the original part of the pub: a space of flagstone floor and stone hearth around which various incarnations of the Raft Pub was attached. At first a simple twelve by twelve single storey place with a hand painted sign outside that, over the years, developed double storey weatherboard grandeur. Although the sisters McDo, which is how they came to abbreviate and represent both names, could barely be seen the regulars of the Raft noticed their presence, either by the clatter of knitting needles, an Ugg booted foot, stretched to the coals, a very rare chortle, May had a particular screech in her laugh, or the grinding of hand axe and block splitter, that in the evening glinted off the fire light.

The sisters McDo cut the firewood every year, split it and carted it, thinned the kindling and set the fire every day it was needed. Oh, and they decided when it was needed. Cutting firewood and lighting a fire was what kept them going at almost 80, despite the onset of arthritis and other ailments of age.

They'd seen their mother carted away into a home at their age, simply because the authorities thought she couldn't look after herself. Which translated into the fact that she smelled a bit and lived in the cold. So Mary and May made a pact to make sure they smelled nice fed themselves and could light a fire.

Both families could trace their presence in Shipwreck back to the raft. The McDonalds always claimed their innocence and that they were fitted up in some sort of Shakespearian conspiracy. The McDougalls, on the other hand, had no problems admitting they led an insurrection against the English landlords clearing the land. Both families did well after washing up in the Valley and succeeded in not just growing orchard fruit but also developing hardy new and improved varieties through careful grafting.

Along the way, both McDonalds and McDougalls had married McDuffs, McCrumbs, McMullans, McMillans and McDillons. Only Wee Al's brother Andrew broke the rules of pip to pip and stone to stone by taking up with Dulcie O'Donnel. "Nothing will come of that" the rest of the family muttered under their breath. But plenty did. Five children, one a distinguished brain surgeon, one doing 15 years for armed robbery and wounding, one farming in NZ, one living in Syria with her former refugee husband helping rebuild the country and the last in an institution for the mentally deranged. Only two of the five were spoken of readily. Big Al and Wee Al, had run the pub for 20 years, having bought it when their families subdivided and sold the orchards, and following a moderately distinguished footy career with one of the Sallyman Cove clubs, retired back to their hometown. Big Al was the brains behind the business. Wee Al, being wee, had spent a bit too much time at the bottom of the pack which showed in his face, particularly his nose, and his mental agility. No one bothered the cousins, as both retained the hard physique, muscle tone and outward confidence that had served them well on the footy field. That they were likely to be the last of their line, didn't bother either. They were happy in each other's company, with a mutual love forged on the sports field.

They ran a tidy bar, never any trouble, even when the end of season piss ups descended on them, or some of the hill folk, usually the women, took umbrage at the pretentiousness of the new flotsam. And they looked after their Mums, who had been deserted, by death and dereliction. The first untimely, Mary's husband crushed beneath a flipped tractor. Death by Massey Ferguson as he roared, a little too fast, down the slope with a laden trailer of firewood. His body was found the next day. It was thought that he died of internal bleeding, before the quolls and devils eviscerated him for the soft meat. There was much mourning and Mary was almost a year grieving.

There was no such sadness when May was deserted. Indeed it was thought well past time, when the rest of the family finally lost patience and May could no longer hide her bruises. Whether Alistair the elder was driven out of town or went of his own accord is not known. It is however known that the scars left on Alistair the younger set him against developing a relationship with a woman for fear he was too much his father's son. Instead, his dedication was poured into footy, where he was a feared opponent in the ruck, and recently running the bar.

❁

Dinghy and Nigel shared the occasional conversation from their respective perches, out front overlooking the bay. Dinghy reclined into a ratty wicker chair, tinny in hand, ash on his trackie pants, a grey trail highlighted against the black of his T shirt, stubby butt almost hidden in the curls of his grey muzzle. He invariably gazed straight ahead contentedly musing at the gentle lap of the bay.

Nigel parked his bony arse on a timber slatted folding chair. The type you find in trendy cafes with matching tables. He'd set both up afresh, having taken them inside when not in use. He crossed one leg over the other, in elegant dangle, a feat Dinghy could never achieve, and poured a wine into a crystal stemmed glass. Always a stem Nigel insisted. His gaze crossed Dinghy's and rested on his 26 foot yacht, *Cock Robin*. Size was important to Nigel, while Dinghy poked fun of his preoccupation with size, telling him he had over 40 foot all added up.

"Still drinking that crap beer," Nigel sniped.

"Yep, all my life. Still drinking that crap wine."

Nigel laughed but didn't reply. His wine came from the wine club he subscribed to, top of the range dozens, delivered every month. He knew Dinghy had no understanding of wine and he had no interest in educating him, while Dinghy had no interest in being educated.

"Been out much lately" Dinghy asked across the driveway that separated them, meaning out on the water.

"Not really, too busy with work" Nigel replied with that tone of responsibility that comes with folk dedicated to the Holy Church of Work.

Truth be known Nigel hadn't been out in six months except to his boat, since he ran into the sisters McDo, outside the post office, and Mary, glancing at him in profile as they passed, hissed to May

"Now there's an O'Donnel nose if ever."

Which May confirmed with an emphatic, "Oh yes." Then added, "and the hairline too, that widow's peak. Well, we know why the old cottage was never on the market now."

"Yes we do sister," and they scuttled back to the Raft.

Dinghy could never work Nigel out. Looked like he had everything he wanted but no time to enjoy it. "Geez, you don't come down here to be busy. I thought you'd retired anyway." He jibed back

"Can't do that mate, got two ex-wives, two teenagers, both useless layabouts, and the current wife and her family to support."

"Bloody hell mate, you're a slave. Haven't you ever wanted to get in that boat of yours and just bugger off, leave 'em to sort it out for themselves?"

"What and do nothing, just sail? You got to be joking. I'd go mad in a week."

"You reckon. Nah you'd find something else." Dinghy finished one beer, crushed the can under his running shoe shod foot, a shoe that had never run anywhere in its three years of being out of the box, and cracked another. He put a paper and worm of baccy in his rolling machine closed the lid, took the cigarette from the slot, lit it and continued. "Have you never done anything else in life, but... what is it? Structural what?"

"Design. It's like architecture but no fancy bits, we just make sure things don't fall down. And no, I haven't."

"Blimey." Dinghy let out a cloud of blue smoke in exasperation.

Nigel poured himself another glass of plonk and answered his phone with a nod to Dinghy. It was work, it was always work.

Dinghy gulped a mouthful of beer, swallowed and mumbled, "Poor sod."

Conversation never really developed more than that. Mutual nods and snipes in passing, a rare smile and shake of the head from Dinghy and a cussing glare and silent grumble at the rusting troop carrier from Nigel. It was pretty much the same all down the street. A village in appearance, but a suburb in exercise. All insular and sideways looks.

Just as Nigel was decamping, four blokes, or "boys" as they referred to themselves, were tying up a little boat across the road and decamping with the day's catch. You could tell they were blokes and fifty years more than boys from the deep and loud tenor of their voices. You could also tell they were long time mates from the ease of their conversation and intimate knowledge of each other's ailments, as well as the familiar "o" attached to three of their names. Which, incidentally, was only used on fishing trips, like they were pirate code names. Two of the four, their jeans and overalls worn soft and comfy like their jumpers, carted a bucket of fish in each hand, the others hauled a plastic tub of gear between them.

"Oy Dinghy, fish supper tonight," one of the blokes with a bucket offered.

"Don't mind if I do. Did alright today then?"

"You bet, Flathead of course, couple of gummy sharks, and Bob snagged a bream on the way back along the shoreline. You know, down near the old jetty."

On the pavement in front of Dinghy's place, Bob lifted his prize fish out his bucket. Among the bottom feeding Flatheads, both eyes atop and to the rear of a hammered down forehead and grey skinned scaleless sharks, the bream stood out as what some would see as the only real fish in the bucket.

"There's a couple of nice flatties for you Dinghy old mate" and Davo, with the other bucket strode up to the veranda where he flapped them in Dinghy's face.

"Get off yer bugger," protested Dinghy, leaning away and almost tipping out of his chair. "Give 'em to Nor."

Dinghy hated the feel of fish, hated their scales, their look, especially Flathead and hated their slime, so he never fished, no matter how much his grandchildren nagged him. But he loved fish and chips, with thick batter, loads of salt and drowned in vinegar, proper dark malt vinegar. Oh, and like he used to remind everyone, "proper chips, chunky like. None of this French fry soggy nonsense."

Jacko with the nets and tackle, who only ever wore khaki overalls, offered Nigel a couple of fresh caught flatty's, "or we could spare a shark if you like mate. Won't get fresher."

Nigel leaned forward to inspect the offerings, as if mildly tempted, before declining. "No thanks. We only buy fish from our man in town." He declined in a voice somewhere between posh grammar school and big spread grazier.

"Not asking yer to buy it, mate. But suit yourself."

The four blokes, Davo, Jacko, Robo and Bob settled down on Dinghy's veranda. Dinghy winched himself from the groaning chair and fetched another six pack. Nigel packed up his chair and table and retired, probably to the office. Davo suggested something about him hiding a bit of Dinghy's driftwood about his anatomy.

The boys finished a beer each then dragged their catch across to the pub, where they found a willing market for most of their fish and received credit at the bar for a pleasurable day's fishing. Big and Wee Al were always keen to put a fish supper on and the Sisters McDo, ensconced in the nook, where they could see everything and curse almost everything that fell outside their perception of normality, like tattoos, especially on women, long hair on men, men getting too close to other men, mixed race couples, or friends, excessive jewellery and skimpy clothing, even certain ways of walking, thought they were the only ones that could do fish supper as it should be done, and their sons, were more than happy to encourage their old fashioned ways, at least in the kitchen, for Big Al knew that the blowins that spent most in the Raft, knew their fine food and had time and money to eat out. It also made them feel more local if they got a whisper about special happenings and both Als got a wee giggle out of folk thinking they'd stumbled upon a hidden gastropub.

❀

The flotsam of the Esplanade and weekend farmers, in the foothills behind, are in many ways and odd ways, with the obvious exception of the Furphys, the lifeblood of Shipwreck and Hidden Valley, despite being largely hunched, overweight, diabetic, with crumbling bones, translucent skin and watery blood. It is because of their very condition, being considerably past their productive prime, not to mention having very little idea of, or the stamina for primary production, or much manual work, that the remaining young folk have work outside the family farm and mountain compounds, building extensions, erecting fences, renovations, mowing lawns, planting and pruning fruit trees, clipping the feet of spoilt pets, shearing alpacas, cutting firewood and cleaning house. All those things and many more that folk born into the countryside learn to do out of necessity.

# Chapter 2

## The House that Jack and Jill Built

At the end of the last century Jack and Jill came to Hidden Valley and built a house. They bought land on the lower side of the western scarp, just out of Shipwreck. Jack dug holes and collected stones and Jill wrangled toddlers and birthed another. When the children were sleeping they both mixed mortar and set out stones, like a neolithic jigsaw puzzle, to make walls. Then they sawed timber, nailed on a roof of shiny tin and fitted out all within.

After they built the house they grew a garden, that grew bigger and bigger each year and fed them more and more each year. On birthdays and pagan festivals they bought each other tools to help manage the garden more easily.

That allowed them to sit more and enjoy where they were more.

Soon they had it working so well they couldn't tell the difference between work and rest. That left them time to play with the children, which meant taking them into the garden to plant vegetables and browse on what was already grown and pick something for dinner. Or they would all go into the bush up the hill, hunt wallaby and collect mushrooms and firewood. On other days they all went fishing. Most of the time the children thought it was fun and, like Jack and Jill, didn't really notice the difference between work and play.

Then along came school. Jack and Jill started home schooling, which worked well for a bit. That was before the oldest, Jack Junior, met other kids and wanted to play footy. Then Jill Junior wanted to meet other kids and then Middleman wanted the same and they all agitated in that nagging way kids agitate. So Jack and Jill gave in and sent them to "proper school", as Jack Junior coined it.

He was the oldest and most pushy. He liked to linger and watch footy matches when they passed a game at the local oval. But Jill wouldn't have any of it, pointing out how dangerous it was and how short Jack Junior was.

He, kind of understood that, even if he didn't like it. Then one day during the summer holiday, on the way back from fishing, he saw kids playing cricket on the beach and coyly asked to join them. That was it, slapping a tennis ball around on the beach for a couple of hours in the sun and Jack Junior had found his first love, and play-work at home just wasn't the most fun anymore.

❋

Pretty soon the nearest paddock to the house was mowed and flattened into his own personal cricket oval, which the rest of the family were invited to share, as long as they bowled and fielded and didn't hog the batting crease.

With this development Jack and Jill discovered a bossy little bugger who, while only eight, thought he could direct everyone to his own desires. Jack blamed Jill for that feature of his character and she, him. After some discussion they loaded the blame onto Jack's Dad, who was not only deeply conservative, but naturally dictatorial.

It all settled down when Middleman—they called him that because he didn't like being second—got big enough to aim a tennis ball, quite fast, at his brother's head. They loved each other and were quite inseparable, to the point they would gang up on Jack, but there always remained a competitive spirit.

Jill Junior really wasn't much chop at ball games. When she was press ganged into fielding she'd get out of the way of the ball if it came near her, or let it bounce before catching it, which really peed Middleman off because he wanted to bat.

To make things a bit more fair, Jack came up with the idea of planting fielders, like scarecrows, around the oval, so if you hit one you were out. At first Jack Jr wasn't too happy, intent on counting higher and higher as he slapped the ball around and wore a furrow in the middle of the paddock.

The only way the children stayed engaged with the way they used to live, was Sundays on the foreshore. There they would forage for mussels and oysters, plucking them from crevices and weedy havens. They pried oysters, both flat Pacific and crinkly Atlantics, escaped from farms across the bay, from their rocks. One bucket of mussels they would wrest from their tide washed homes and often a dozen oysters would be snacked for lunch.

Together with the honey harvest it was the one activity that preserved through teenage years. Then the children grew big enough to move away and soon lost sight of where they lived and any sense of how they lived.

As the children grew, so the garden grew and soon gave them everything they needed. Fruit and veg and honey, even medicine. Jill became known as the woman to go to for cures for whatever ailed you, or whatever you thought you needed. To say that Jill was on intimate terms with her garden is a huge understatement. She knew, not only where every plant grew, when it grew, when it flowered, when it seeded, insects it harboured and nutrients it needed, she also knew what it was good for and in some cases what caution was needed in its company. It was as if she communicated with each individual plant. Not in that mad old woman way but in the same way a good teacher makes an effort to get to know every child in class.

Like children some were good and easy to be with, others needed more work to get them to flourish. Some bloomed near the window, others closer to hand. Some bore only good, while in others malevolence fruited. It was indeed her own children that deepened her engagement with the plants she tended. Herbs at the back door, trees and vegetables further afield. She learned to enquire and discover features in most plants that were unknown to most.

The simple onion, often fried and occasionally boiled, was the first to reveal its greater depth, via a small snippet in a homespun hippy type magazine.

When the children came down with a ticklish and persistent cough, one of those things children share often, she discovered that cut raw and steeped in warm honey, the modest bulb soothed better than mixture blended by large pharmaceutical companies, and that dosage was as required and that once Jack and Jill and Middleman got over the odd combination, they would dip into the jar on the side of the stove, even as the cough seemed to be disappearing. What neither Jill or Jack realised though was that even natural remedies have side effects and that while the children's collective throats were soothed, the cough erupted with a flatulent blast below.

Soon Jill was blending balms for sunburn, and grazes, teas for upset stomachs, lotions for acne and eventually oils and distillations for congestion, headaches and any other ailment. When there was no honey to harvest the little shed at the back of the house oozed with the scent of various drying leaves and flowers and spirits and potions, that were ground and labelled in small brown jars or blended into creamy pastes and stacked on shadowy shelves out of the light. More concentrated brews were carefully filtered into even smaller vials with dippers and pin head screw tops, then locked away in a remote, almost hidden drawer.

Jack Junior was the main recipient of his mother's craft. He was the child that seemed to bring home or invent most minor illnesses or incur most minor injuries. The type of thing a good rub or the placebo effect of a sticky plaster would fix. Jill's ointment for bruises was his favourite, probably because it smelled good. As a result it wasn't long before Jill's bruise cream found its way into the cricket club first aid kit and she received requests from other mothers of children bearing bruises or muscle strains.

While Jill was flattered by the popularity of her balm, she was also a little embarrassed and found herself in a tricky spot. You see, sale of such beneficial goods is overregulated for one, and met with a dubious or sceptical reception. While she often cursed that all she was doing was relieving suffering, she found that such a worthy cause had been sucked into the domain of licensed practitioners and they got very pissed off when any, in particular a woman of knowledge, common sense and dedication to a craft stepped on their toes.

At first it upset her as she was convinced that her applications (I'd like to call them medicines but you know how things are) were useful and relieved suffering, but gradually she became content to treat the family and friends and friends of friends by way of swapping and trading fruit and veg with those who had something to swap and trade. That mostly meant the folk of the hills who hunted, trapped, grew and foraged things and made things from what they hunted, trapped, grew or foraged. While some along the foreshore believed in the effectiveness of her balms and potions, Jack and Jill had no need for financial counsellors, as they didn't need or have much money, relationship counsellors, as they had a perfectly good relationship and always talked out any hitches, and their lifestyle was, to them, uncomplicated and perfect, so no coaching was needed and neither were musically inclined.

Anyway by the time the children left home, which in each case was before they turned twenty, as a result of Jack and Jill filling their heads with all the wonders of the world and places and adventures they'd seen before they settled in Hidden Valley, Jill had a cream, balm, lotion or potion for pretty much everything, all drawn from her extensive garden and was now exploring the various native plants up the hill. In many ways her further explorations filled the gap left by the children when they set out on their own adventures. Jack simply went fishing more and together they joked that they should have had more children to increase the chances of one staying around to help on the farm, or at least kept them dumb and not filled their imaginations with wonder.

As Jill found more time to devote to her balms and potions, her tinctures took on an ever more intense form. She gradually reduced them into powerful droplets, decanted into tiny bottles, swaddled in fur lined boxes or leather pouches.

❁

In the years to come, the garden, which was almost a farm by then, with cows and goats in the paddocks, chickens and ducks in the back yard, geese patrolling the driveway, and a couple of black and tan mongrels supervising everything from the veranda, gave more than they needed. So they took a lot of stuff to swap with others, people who were starting out, and mostly gave it away.

Every other week Jack would load up the ute with vegetables that were in season, like tomatoes, celery, cabbage, carrots and corn. He'd also put in a couple of cheeses if they had spare and Jill would do up bundles of herbs and jars of honey, and away they would go to a little park in an outlying village.

There they would meet others and set out what they had to swap. Other folk would mostly come down from the hills, and bring fruit and veg, and sometimes fish or meat, fresh and dried. There was no formal value given to anything. People simply offered things in return for what they wanted and, for at least half the year, everyone that came went home with more variety than they came with and never spent a cent and had enough food to last a week or more.

They also talked about how they grew it, caught it, raised it or made it. Jack loved listening to fishing tips and Jill was always happy to talk gardening, especially herbs and bees. Together they talked goats and cheese, but what they loved most about it was old fashioned trading and bartering and tasting the food that other folks, friends, had grown and knowing it was grown well.

❁

As Jack and Jill grew older and older they didn't grow as much, or harvest as much. Jack struggled to get the boat in and out of the water on his own and his friends, who often helped him began to fall away. At first they suggested Jack sell the old wooden dinghy and get one of those lightweight aluminium, tinny things most blokes had. But Jack would have none of that, admonishing "that the settlers came here in wooden boats and he'd go out in a wooden boat."

At which point the old crew, Davo, Robo and Bob, relented. Also aware that Jack had repaired it so many times that it had become like family to him and getting to know another boat wasn't going to happen, especially one that really took care of itself.

The hives were a big effort for Jill too. So while Jack's boat saw more time tied up to a tree down at the beach, the hives and all the bee gear was gradually packed away in the shed, with only one hive remaining in the garden. Eventually the grass grew long, the fruit trees reached unrulily for the sky. The paddocks were almost empty, except for one old brown goat, that Jill squeezed enough milk out of for their cereal every morning and discussed the state of the world with, and an equally old donkey that she increasingly mistook for Jack.

By now they didn't eat as much from the garden. Partly because the garden didn't seem to give as much and partly because they simply didn't eat as much. But it didn't stop Jill spending most of her time squatting between weeds and herbs, stepping around toadstools and other surprises that popped out of the ground at different times of the year.

Actually the garden did give lots, but mostly fed the wildlife, which Jack and Jill didn't mind, because they figured they'd eaten enough wallaby in their time, that it was okay to give something back.

Then Jill started to forget where things were, what things were and who Jack was. More and more Jack was having to get her in from the goat shed, where he found her talking to Brian the donkey like he was Jack, while she spoke to Jack like he was her brother, who died many years ago.

She still knew her herbs and most things in the garden. They were, in many ways the anchor that kept her grounded. So too the plants of the bush up the hill, where Jack would also quite often have to call her back from. Jill was indeed a library of plants and their uses. The problem was the catalogue was getting muddled.

❀

One warm Autumn morning, just after the sun had burnt off the fog and banished it back down to the foreshore, Jill went into the garden to gather food for lunch. Jack made a flask of tea and they packed a picnic to take up the hill. Jack had just about finished cutting the firewood for the following year and was cleaning up for a small burn. For the last ten years they'd been burning off small parcels of the land, following the advice of a local fellow, that lived over the back of their place in an old bus and advised small, low cold burns as a way of managing the land. Both Jack and Jill enjoyed lighting little fires and felt they were doing the land good. So much so they made regular picnics of the occasion and always stayed to watch over it.

Jill packed a freshly gathered salad, leaves plucked and pulled, snapped from stems and they took some of the pie from last night's dinner. Jack also liked to take what he called a "warmer" to spice up the tea. They reached the crest of the hill in good time, from where they could see right down the valley and out into the bay, even through the light smoke that almost surrounded them.

Like settlers from a biscuit tin lid painting, they squatted on a log in front of a little welcoming fire. They ate pie, and they sipped at the steaming brew from clear glasses.

Jack poured a dram of the green into his tea and they both marvelled at the slow mixing with the yellowish tea. He offered some to Jill, in that familiar just checking way that intimate couples do. "Yes," she said, and they watched it melding again.

He turned and went to kiss her on the lips and she pushed him away and punched him. "Don't. Brother and sister don't kiss on the lips."

Jack leaned forward then put his arm around Jill and Jill, fumbling a minuscule leather bag that swung from a thong around her neck, told him,

"Tell Mum I am going away with Jack because he loves me." And she eased a tiny glass vial from the tiny pouch.

Jack hesitated, as if to say "are your sure" but uttered nothing. She tipped two tiny drops of red liquid into her tea and passed it back to Jack. He put the lid on it and they both marvelled again as the red disappeared into the yellow green of Jill's tea.

Jack smiled and they reclined. He wrapped his coat around Jill and spooned in. He squeezed her tight, rubbed her leg, stroked her belly, then cupped her breast. She placed her hand over the back of his and held it closer and they gazed through the smoke, out to the bay for a long time, until, with a shudder, the cold fell.

A change of wind wafted the smoke back at them. Jack's eyes smarted and recognising the fire was low he raked it closer to where they lay, making a circle, stoking it with more wood, mostly fresh, the leaves from the treetops, building a bower.

The air filled with that tell-tale eucalyptus aroma. He stacked it higher than normal and raked it in even closer, retreating as it grew. Flames leapt higher than two men and as the flames grew the smoke dissipated and the aroma changed. Jack's eyes smarted less but remained streaky damp. He watched over the fire all afternoon, before taking a lonely walk down the hill at last light.

Jack was expected the next day. Second Saturday of every month the boys, as they called themselves, met. Jack spoke to Jill like he always used to when she was away. Imagined her at her mother's, or eating exotic food in squishy dusty cafes with old friends. He occasionally and briefly wondered what they talked about, usually while making coffee or stoking the oven.

Then smiled and considered how lucky he was that Jill was probably saying nice things about him and then that whatever they talked about was nothing to do with him and again how lucky he was that Jill was Jill and how he loved her history too.

He slopped on his ratty shirt, well past it's best, ripped off sleeves, frayed collar, hardly a button. Jill had refused to sew any back on. Jack wasn't sure if it was a feminist thing, or if she thought the shirt was ripe for the bin. She had an ambiguous way sometimes that he loved, simply because it kept him guessing and only sometimes pissed him off.

Khaki overalls, plimmies, a well-known tyre brand, formerly white, now grungy grey with holes and sandy streaks and he was ready. He'd worn the same shoes since he was a teenager and the same overalls since he developed a paunch. The rest of his clothes lived in the back of the ute. He said goodbye to Jill, just before closing the ute door, that needed a good slam to stay shut. Sometimes Jill was squatting in the garden, camouflaged among berry plants or brassicas, usually with Jammy in close attendance, digging where he wasn't supposed to, but thinking he was helping. But today she wasn't there and old Jammy had just slipped into the cab before the door slammed.

Davo and Robo were waiting at the boat. Davo had further to come, down from the mountains, way out the back of Sourtree. He'd grown up there in a big old mud brick mansion his Californian, proto hippy folks built in the sixties and it was now his that he shared with a regular female visitor. Davo was never late and always picked up Robo on the way through, even though it was a bit of detour.

Robo was the newest boy and probably the most remote in that he lived on the edge of the Lost West, up the windiest of tracks, the type that get tourists chucking a quick uey. Most of the time Robo was stoned and writing poetry. Not quite retired but close enough to take a chance living on a small part time income and invest everything he and Kathy had in trying to be self-sufficient up the sharp end of a valley, where it seemed like every river began. They were seven years in and coming to realise how much they loved living small, buying nothing, eating really well from what they grew, fattened, and caught and the rest of the time doing what they wanted.

Mostly those things they'd been denied when working and bringing up kids.

The fourth of the boys, Bob, no o, was always late. He didn't have as far to come so set off after he saw, or heard, Davo's knackered Land Rover clunk by.

Bob also brought a thermos of the best coffee and the later he came the hotter it stayed.

They each carried a boat rod and preferred bait or lures, for a bit of friendly competition. Jack and Bob seemed to get most fish most days. Davo really didn't have much idea, and Robo was usually stoned just enough so he didn't care. No matter who caught the most fish it was shared.

The tide was rising to its peak on the way out and the four men rowed hard against the current. Once at the buoy that marked their favourite spot coffee with a little brandy was taken. Soon the fish started biting. They hauled in a couple of couple of gummy sharks and half a dozen cocky salmon. Jack saw the salmon come in on Bob's line and knew most were for him as the other boys didn't like the brown flesh and they knew Jill loved it.

Drifting in they set their rods for Flatheads. Robo hit a patch first and snagged four in two casts for the first time ever. After that he got nothing and the other boys filled their buckets one at a time. Each fish measured against the size of the boy's boot. Which was unfortunate for Bob, as his feet were the biggest, so he tossed more fish back than most.

On the way in Jack could see smoke still rising from the highest point. He knew that was his place.

❁

Jack set the table for two and soused the cocky salmon in herb vinegar, as he always did. They both liked the tang it gave the firm brown flesh. He ate his with bread and butter, lots of butter and washed it down with a home-brewed stout. He sat at the table for a long time, silent, then ate the fish he'd prepared for Jill, pulled the heads from the skeletons and put them in Jammy's bowl.

"Just you and me old fella. More fish tomorrow?"

Jammy set about polishing his bowl and Jack shifted to the old style computer on a kid's desk in the corner, turned it on, penned an email and sat motionless in front it. He clicked on Jill's email address, then poured himself a small whisky from the special reserve that lived behind the couch.

There were twelve bottles, each half full. They only came out on special days and were added to each year on Jack's birthday. Always a previously unknown bottle of single malt. Always taken with teaspoon of water. Jack was particular about that.

He sat back down and began to write to Jill, telling her about fishing and how much he missed her, and how he was looking forward to seeing her soon. He hit send, took a deep swallow and set to write to the children. At the back of his mind, he knew he had to and started to write with exhaustive depth, in that way authors tease the reader before finally getting to the point He then scrapped it and simply wrote:

> *Mum's gone up the hill*
> *Tomorrow I'll go fishing*
> *And we'll wave goodbye.*
>
> Love Mum and Dad

Then next day Jack looked out at the long grass falling over and how the fruit trees had grown into each other, so they looked like a fruit medley hedge. He looked at the fences falling down, at the goat and donkey trying to sneak through the bit patched up with sticks woven through the remaining wire. "I'll get on to that soon love," he said, as he had been saying for the last year.

As he peered out the windows he wasn't sure if he was seeing through spider webs or cataracts. Then Jammy nuzzled his wet mongrel snout in for a pat.

Jack called him to the old ute. He hopped up into the well of the passenger seat, then onto the seat itself.

Old Jammy was almost fifteen, that's a hundred and forty five in dog years, Tub had died a couple of years back, probably because she was the biggest of the two and got most the food, unless Jack or Jill was watching, and was buried under the foxgloves, where she seemed to like to bury her bones.

Jammy had lost one ear as a result of digging up another dog's bone stash. A normally docile Labrador, even with small children poking fingers in orifices, had taken offence to this upstart mongrel that came for a visit and started helping herself, so ripped off Jammy's left ear in a pretty quick, one-sided melee. Jill was horrified, but Jack, after tending to the wound, along with the Lab's apologetic owner, reckoned that if he'd walked in and straight away helped himself to the special reserve whisky, he'd have been due at least a clip around the ear. Jammy got over it and was none the worse, apart from looking a bit off balance. And Jack often got a dram of twenty year old single malt on subsequent visits, while Jammy and Tub were perfect guest.

At the foreshore, Jack helped the old dog into the boat, as he always did, and heaved it into the bay. It was a big effort but the tide was in his favour, and he thought of the boys telling him to trade it in for something lighter as it scuffed across the sand. He rowed gently, for the best part of an hour, to the spot where he fished. From there most of the houses on the foreshore blurred into one thin strip. It was always when fishing from this spot that looking back at the land he understood why some folk never left. It was a whole different world from a small boat and with each passing year the shapes became distant impressions, the furthest being the summit of his land, where today the last wisp of grey smoke greeted his gaze.

The returning tide washed Jack's boat up onto the beach. Only Jammy's constant yapping brought it to people's attention. Dinghy secured it before phoning Bob.

# Chapter 3

## Blowins

Pretty soon a man in a suit put a sign up outside Jack and Jill's place. And pretty soon a big shiny station wagon pulled up out the front. The sign came down and John-Jack, or JJ, as he liked to be called and Gill, short for Gillianna, moved in.

They'd fallen in love with the olde worlde charm of stone and weatherboards and wrinkly roof and all the funny old sheds, strange tools and ancient farming gear that Gill just knew would make lovely garden sculptures.

They both loved the idea of living in the country, with all that peace and quiet and keeping animals. They weren't so keen on the spiders and snakes and long grass but would soon take care of them.

JJ was thin, with soft hands, soft beard and neat long red hair. They were the same height, five foot six. Gill also had soft hands, was soft in those places women are and had black hair falling around a stern face, even when smiling. Gill was in love with JJ and he with her, and Gill also loved the whole country home and garden aesthetic, which she displayed in her well-known rural outfitter's attire. Including wide brimmed Gillaroo hat.

The local folk welcomed JJ and Gill and offered lots of advice on what to grow, what to keep, fences that needed mending, and where to get this and that. Mostly they just wanted to have a squiz and vet their new neighbours, who had moved into what would still be known as Jack and Jill's place, much to the displeasure of JJ and Gill.

The first thing the new owners did, after wiping down all the surfaces and scrubbing the bathroom and kitchen, was explore the old sheds, which were packed to the very threshold, floor to ceiling, with old and new tools and thingamajigs they had no idea about.

Soon they realised there was quite a bit to do to fix up the old place. A bit more than dusting and polishing. So, following lots of fiddling with his phone and computer and a dusty old plastic box with flashing lights old Jill had installed at the nagging of the children, JJ explored the local social media page, *HV Community*, and at the request of Gill, he left a message.

*Window cleaner wanted must be reliable.*

Sure enough, he got a couple of replies and the next day a young lad pulled into the yard on a noisy old trail bike with a bucket and sponge.

Gill greeted him cautiously, a little perplexed by his tattoos and earrings and other studs in various appendages. Serving her coffee was one thing, but cleaning her windows and peering into her house was quite different.

He asked for some water and explained that his squeegee must have fallen out of the bucket on his way here and did she have one he could borrow.

Gill told him there was probably one in the shed and pointed the way. Soon every window was gleaming and not a dead spider in sight. She paid the lad and he left happily with his bucket, sponge and a new squeegee.

Next they decided to do something about the garden. One of the neighbours had mentioned snakes on the move this time of year and how important it was to keep the grass short. That had put the willies up the pair of them. So JJ posted another message, and the next day another young lad rolled up in a rusty old ute, with an equally rusty old mower.

"Morning Mrs, I'm here to do your lawn."

"Morning" said Gill, a little more relaxed at the clean cut, boy-next-door appearance of this particular lad. "I'm Gill."

"Oh, like the old girl that used to live here."

"No. Gill-with-a-G," she replied curtly.

"Oh, okay. I'm Pete with a P," said the mower man. The last part as he turned to start the mower.

Five times he pulled the cord, before giving up and explaining that he'd have to go home and fix it but could come back tomorrow.

Gill-with-a-G desperately wanted the grass cut. Her fear of snakes was turning into paranoia. So she gestured to the shed.

A couple hours later Pete had the lawn tamed. There were a few bald patches, but it was safe and Gill-with-a-G was relieved, duly paid Pete, then slipped back inside, out of the heat.

Pete packed up his old mower, his rake and shiny new mower and slipped away. While Gill-with-a-G admired her trim lawn through her gleaming windows.

JJ had spent most of the time in what used to be the honey house, pulling his hair out. Well, really pulling at wires, but his ginger top knot was falling out.

The honey house, a small shed about 3x3 was a quaint little construction.

Perfectly sealed and lined, insect screens on the solitary window and door, completely empty and most of all cool. Which JJ thought would be ideal for his supersize computer screens and make long hours staring at them more comfortable than in the house.

Like many other folk who had drifted to the country recently, JJ worked remotely, and he was determined to make the former honey house his office, from where he could write code and fix things most folk in Shipwreck had barely heard of. The problem was JJ couldn't fix the internet so he could get a signal in the honey house, which previously only had one light switch, one socket, and was built in a nice shady hollow, between the garden and paddock.

He was getting more and more irritated when he admitted he was going to have to put in a cable. So he measured up the distance—six metres, went back to the house and posted another message:

*Trench digger wanted*

*to dig 6 metre trench*

*Must be reliable*

Sure enough, the next day old Bob knocked on the door, spade in hand.

"G'day mate, I'm Bob. Where do you want your trench."

JJ showed him the path. Bob pushed back his beer brand cap and shook his head. "Hard ground that, compacted. You wouldn't have a pick and bar I could use, would you?"

JJ looked into space. "A what?"

"Pickaxe and iron bar. I'll need to crack the surface and there's bound to be some rock down there. Always is, just where you don't want it. I expect you'll want it 600.

"How much?"

"Deep." Bob laughed, his gut rolling. "I can do it for $300, have it knocked over in a day or so, depending on floaters."

"Floaters?"

"Rocks mate, big buggers. So pick and bar?"

JJ gestured to the shed. Then went back into the house to work from the kitchen table.

At the end of day a sweaty Bob, his overalls damp and elastic sided work boots caked in yellow mud, collected his $300, gathered his spade, pick axe and bar and toddled off home, via the pub, where he parked his tools at the door, banged his boots cleanish, but still left a slight trail on the floor, pulled up a bar stool next to Pete with a P and ordered a beer from a tattooed and jewelled bar man.

"G'day Bob. Knocked off for the day?"

"Yep. 'spect I'll be back in a few days to fill it in."

Your round Son?" He said with sideways nudge.

At the end of the week Bob filled in the trench and trousered another $300.

❈

JJ was now ensconced in his new office, where he spent ten, sometimes twelve hours a day. You see JJ was the type of fellow who thought the world would collapse without his input. Which was probably why his hair line had receded to where his man bun lifted from almost the centre of his skull.

In the house Gill was decorating. To be honest she was scratching out thumbnail sketches, moving stuff around, draping bits of cloth over chairs and sticking colour swatches on walls with blu tack. But she called it decorating in the same way a lot of folk called buying an empty block of land and getting someone to construct a house on it, "owner building".

At supper time, which was when JJ thought the world could survive for the evening without him, probably because he thought most folk were asleep, Gill told him they needed a builder and then a tiler and then a decorator.

JJ still had a head full of code that no one but he understood and wasn't that interested, responded tersely, "We have a perfectly nice house, I thought you loved this house just the way it was. You said it had so much character, warmth and wonderful history."

Gill countered, and following a short one way discussion, she agreed to find a builder tomorrow when she went into the village.

Gill needed a few bits and pieces from the shop while she was looking for a builder, so popped into Clancy's. At the head of the laundry and cleaning products aisle she paused, basket to the fore like the bumper of the old Volvo she drove, shielding her from oncoming people. In this case however the plastic coated wire mesh was as effective as a pushchair in a collision with the aforementioned bumper.

She teetered on the threshold. About two metres away, oddly hunched over the shampoo, yet swaying back at the same time, was a young lad in greasy jeans and knitted jumper with more holes than thread. His hair brown and shoulder length, plastered to his skull. She teetered a little closer, aiming at the shampoo herself then pulled back.

"Don't mind Flathead, he's harmless," advised the short, over inflated shopkeeper.

It wasn't, however, the sight of the lad that retarded Gill's progress. Since being taken aback at the ornamentation of the window cleaner she'd made a point not to show her surprise at the odd appearance of local folk. It was much more, as she tried to communicate to the shopkeeper with a sour mouth and twitching nose, the stench surrounding her fellow shopper.

She retreated to the counter and introduced herself, to which the round and bouncing shopkeeper replied, "I'm Clancy. This is my place. Anything you want, just ask."

Gill gestured over her shoulder and pulled another face.

Clancy leaned in, just a little too close for Gill's liking, "They get a bit pongy from time to time the mountain folk. We don't see them that often to worry. They come in once a month on average. Coincides with their dole. Usually just soap, laundry and station rations, flour, sugar and tea and coffee. Don't know what else they eat. Can't grow much up there."

Gill took a sudden step to the side, sensing an impending presence approaching. "After you." She accompanied the step with, then made a second retreating motion.

Flathead plonked a sack of flour, two kilo of sugar, a six pack of soap and box of teabags on the counter. "That's all today thanks."

Clancy, with a smidgen of mischief, introduced Gill to Flathead. "She's just moved into old Jack and Jill's place." Flathead extended a hand, Gill looked, hesitated, looked to Clancy and shook briefly. "Pleased to meet you," chirped Flathead. "So you're Jill too, that's funny."

"Gill-with-a-G", replied Gill-with-a-G. Which made Flathead and Clancy laugh.

I'm Flathead," replied Flathead. "Charlie really but everyone calls me Flathead. We're almost neighbours, I'm up and over the hill from your place. If you walk up through the bush you'll find us. Used to see old Jill up there quite often, and Jack when he was cutting firewood."

Gill did her best not to show the tensing of her entire being and gave the generic reply, "Pleased to meet you... Flathead."

Once Flathead had paid, she collected her bibs and bobs and picked Clancy's brains. "Are they all like that in the hills and does he really live near us?"

Clancy, being the self-appointed Mayor, was happy to relate what he knew. Which, as far as he was concerned, was all anyone needed to know.

"Flathead's from the bludgers up in the hills, Circus Hill we call it. God knows how many of them are up there. They breed like flies, come and go as they please and live in places you wouldn't keep a dog in. Came down in the 70s and 80s most of 'em. Called themselves alternative farmers, in receipt of the alternative farmers subsidy that they collected once a fortnight."

"Then there's the new lot. Blowins. At least they spend and present well. Most are alright. Some stay, some leave after a winter, some come and go with the seasons. They're pretty useless at being country folk, but they've got the cash to pay someone else to do for them."

It became clear, quite quickly to Gill, that the folk in the hills were lowdown on Clancy's list of desirables, while blowins, such as her and JJ, weren't much better, unless they spent money. As she left the shop Gill began to realise the benefits of shopping online and she wondered if the post mistress might be less prejudicial. Or the delivery man, who seemed to have all the business for hauling goods over the Cold Shoulder, might be more invisible.

There were half a dozen builders' cards on the noticeboard outside, muddled in with yoga classes, garage sales, lost kittens, babysitter adverts, music and art lessons and various therapists. Gill soon settled on one with an eastern cursive frill around the edges of the card that read Valley Builders. She phoned and left a message.

❁

The Post Office was a couple of doors down, between the butchers and a former bank, that like most small towns had been through various incarnations as *Ye Olde Bank Cafe*. Every year or so someone new would come to town, who thought they could cook, and open *Ye Olde Bank Cafe*, with their own personal spin, like muffins, pasties, or channelling their grandmother's ethnic cuisine, and at the end of every summer it would close down. It was currently empty.

Carol, the post mistress, greeted Gill with a smile that beamed nothing but recently discovered confidence. Physically she was as average as they come, height, weight, hair, eyes, even her clothes, neutral uniform like. She even described herself as average. Carol had been post mistress for the last ten years, but one year ago her husband left for a recently arrived yoga teacher. It was messy and left Carol thoroughly deflated, feeling much less than average. At times like that, small towns can get too close, and almost suffocate when everyone knows your very public business and your business is very public.

Then along came Carol. Yes, another Carol, almost six foot tall, the rear of a sprinter, the front of a marathon runner, chestnut hair and skin and dead straight teeth, American straight. This Carol had been posted to the primary school, having impressed at her last school and getting to choose Hidden Valley Primary. She connected well with her students, who all loved her.

Carol lifted Carol from her moonful malaise, simply by talking and listening, and listening and not talking. Carol and Carol were soon firm friends, cycling and canoeing together. Dining regularly together, when the cafe next door was occupied, or at the pub, and within six months Carol had moved into Carol's place at the back of the Post Office, which no one gave any mind to, whether it was more than best friends or not. They were mostly just pleased to get their parcels with a smile again.

❁

The next day a young man, with tatts, metal hanging out of fleshy lobes and gristly parts, knocked on the door. Gill was not quite as taken aback this time. "So you build as well as clean windows?"

"Sure do, also do mechanics and did a couple of years at art school too, before I got jack of it and went to TAFE. I'm Shiv, by the way, short for Shiva.

"Shiv," Gill repeated.

"Yeh hippy parents washed up here via India in the 80s."

Gill directed Shiv into the kitchen and explained, with the effusive gusto of a hyperactive child, where she wanted what colour, talking splash backs and tiling.

Shiv said he didn't do tiles but had a mate that did. She then talked about a kitchen island and a new sink. Again, Shiv said he didn't do sinks but had another mate that was a plumber. They arranged a time to start and talked price. Which Gill quickly agreed to, thinking she had a bargain, compared to what it cost to renovate the little galley kitchen in the inner city terrace they'd moved from.

JJ, meanwhile was commuting a little over six meters a day, five, sometimes six days a week to keep the world moving and society on an even keel. There was no one else to fix a program glitch without him. Without which the next financial meltdown could be just around the corner. Besides someone had to pay for the renovations.

On each journey, JJ passed by the big shed and the small shed. Just like a proper commute, starring out the window of a crowded train, or stuck in traffic, he mused about what was in there, what happened in there. One day he would venture away from his paid path.

Shiv rolled up a few days later with Pete with a P. "This is Pete he's a mate and... "

"Yes we've met, Pete also mows lawns," Gill interrupted. "So you build as well?"

"A bit but mostly I'm a plumber, you know sinks and taps, pipes and toilets. Most round here are builders."

"Oh, that's handy. Now I have a new sink, brass taps, bespoke cupboards and marble bench top arriving tomorrow. They're coming all the way from Sydney. The tiles will be a bit later because they are a special one-off line, being made by a ceramicist, that's a potter, and he's very famous. So if you can have this all out and ready for tomorrow it would be great. I don't want mess hanging around."

Shiv and Pete had the old kitchen ripped out in a day. With the use of pinch bar and a few other tools, borrowed from the shed out back.

They loaded it carefully on the back of the ute. All neatly tied down. Not for the local tip, but to be recycled into a little shack Pete was building up in the hills.

A lot of folk thought there were probably more shacks in the bush than proper houses. Most thought that was alright, as most locals couldn't afford proper houses anymore, so lived in caravans on remote blocks or built shacks or cabins up in the hills, deep in the woods, away from prying eyes. But there were some who thought everything should be done by the book. So people didn't talk about shacks much.

The kitchen cupboards arrived the next day. Shiv and Pete fixed them in place. Again with the help of a nice drill, drill set, and other tools, borrowed from the shed out back.

"All the way from Germany, German Oak that is." Said Gill, proudly running a damp cloth over one of the doors to remove the finger marks Shiv had left on it. "It's almost a hundred years old, recycled from an old wooden ship."

Shiv and Pete shared a smirk. There was a loaded silence, while they thought if they should tell Gill that some of the best timber in the world can be found up in the hills nearby. Pete was about to open his mouth when Shiv suggested they unpack the bench top.

"Careful with that, it's Italian Marble. All the way from... "

"Italy," chimed in the two builders.

The marble bench top fitted perfectly. Gill knew how to order stuff online and she knew interiors, having worked in one of those craft decorator shops that sold knickknacks to give a little bit of a country cottage feel to inner city terraces and apartments.

Pete fitted the sink the next day and plumbed it in with the help of a couple of wrenches, borrowed from the shed. Shiv fixed the splash board and all that remained was the tiling. That would be another week, as the ceramicist had only just shipped them from outback NSW, where, Shiv and Pete learned, he'd made them from hand dug clay and fired them in his wood fired kiln.

The following day Pete hauled his new kitchen up to the shack. His old Holden ute handled the load and the roads easily, benefiting from the weight over the back wheels. Most folk wouldn't attempt the road without a 4 x4 but Pete had grown up negotiating these roads in old bangers Bob had handed down.

His shack was pretty tidy, recycled weatherboards, of at least four different colours and mismatched windows with glass that wobbled everything outside. The roof also spoke of more than one previous owner. He'd rammed a couple of bush poles in the ground to support a veranda of sorts, chucked a few rough sawn slabs down and plonked the ubiquitous old couch outside: ratty, leather look vinyl and yellowing foam busting through.

It wasn't unusual to smell smoke in the air, up in the hill, even in summer. A lot of hill folk cooked with fire all year, either in simple stone hearths or stoves fashioned from 44 gallon drums or mud, or both. Many also burnt small patches of land, often.

Flathead had been burning the ground since he could stand. He learnt from his father, a thin man that meditated on nature, trapped and hunted nature, consumed it and wrote and sang about it, accompanied by a small blond, but burnished guitar, that sounded like old scratchy analogue records. His rhythm mostly set by things dripping over the sink, or the spinning wheel and other hand ranked machines his willowy wife worked around the homestead. There was smoke today and Flathead was watching over it.

Flathead was the nearest neighbour and mate of Shiv and Pete's. They got to know him from working on Pete's shack. Flathead's family drove an old bus onto the block, about twenty five years ago. Flathead was born in it a year later. They should have gone to school together but Flathead's folk were down on the education system so home schooled him. Which, along with basic maths and English, meant he learnt a lot of building skills helping mum and dad put a barn up over the old bus, along with an extensive knowledge of hunting and foraging and skinning and tanning. All of which gave Flathead the skills to build his own room in the corner of the barn and feed and clothe himself.

While Flathead was well equipped with those practical skills, he was less prepared in many other ways and with legs that seemed always slightly bent, a rigid straight back, up until the base of the neck, then a gaze cast forever downward. Unless they were small children he was always looking up at other people, past a broad brow, like the fish commonly hooked in the shallows of the bay. Flathead's posture also made his limbs appear oversized, which, to everyone's surprise, he moved with immense elasticity.

He didn't attract many friends, so tended to cling to Shiv and Pete whenever he ran into them.

Shiv and Pete, kind of looked after Flathead when he came to town, which wasn't too often, as, like his folks and most of the folk on the hill, he kept himself to himself, survived on what he could hunt, grow or forage and by and large had no need, or desire, for the trappings of so called civilisation, such as computers, mobile phones, flushing toilets or hot showers.

In return Flathead lent a hand with building Pete's shack and kept an eye on the place when Pete, and most often Shiv, weren't there. And when they were there, he helped out with the wallaby harvest and processing, that Shiv and Pete derived a modest income from.

✦

There were basically two types of folk that settled up on, what those in the valley called, Circus Hill. The name given to it for the number of performers, artists, and as some said, freaks, who had set up camp on the windward slopes.

They were the religious and the irreligious. The first were recognisable from their long beards and most definitely "their" women in equally long dresses and hair to match. Productive and resolutely independent, The Brethren, as they referred to themselves, shunned all government intervention in their life, or assistance.

The irreligious also did a decent line in full beards, but did not treat women as chattels, indeed many had countered the conventions of conventional society and passed on the matriarchal family name or cobbled together hyphenated tags. They were also much less formal in their attire, doing away with clothing altogether when the climate permitted. Considerate ones posting signs at the bottom of the drive warning of naked folk. They were resolutely independent of thought, but not of income, having no qualms in claiming what they referred to as the "alternative farmers' subsidy", many, but not all arguing that society, as it existed, was utterly corrupt and it was the duty of anyone with revolutionary ideals to hamstring the government by drawing as much as they could to slow its greed and rush to doom.

Others were just happy to live small and grow a bit of dope to sell on to the new liberal folk down in the valley who had never grown anything in their life. What bound the irreligious together was performing. Anything from music, to juggling, fire breathing, singing, performance poets, acrobats, contortionists, a couple of women even strung up a trapeze complete with safety net.

Unlike the Brethren, who had often acquired the skills of milling, carpentry or horticulture before settling on the hill, the circus folk came only with a unique perspective of how to tackle the task of making a shelter and growing food. Yet alongside each other they flourished on the fringes, both feeling society was fucked, but both venturing occasionally into the mainstream.

Flathead's folks were somewhere in between. Not revolutionaries or long bearded Christians who believed work took them closer to God. They were just folk that loved living with nature and being left alone to find their own way.

Pete's shack was, as noted, pretty tidy. The bench and sink fitted snuggly along the back wall, propped on a basic frame. A five gallon bucket caught the wastewater from the sink and a hose from a header tank filled it. Beside the draining board a further bench, propped on milk crates, supported a double burner camp stove that Pete mostly brewed coffee on.

Flathead must have detected the brew and called out as he approached, "G'day—G'day." Pete drained the coffee into a third cup and pointed to his new acquisition. Flathead was impressed and they made plans to harvest some wallaby come dusk.

Gill lavished much care on the new marble surface. She then unpacked a few kitchen necessities from, an until then, still packed box and spent hours shuffling them around, like chess pieces, to get that just right balance. She then moved them again, added some more kitchen object d'art, until there was barely room to butter a slice of toast. Which was okay, as dinner usually came from the microwave perched on top of the fridge, because she hadn't worked out how to use the slow combustion stove and didn't have any wood. Besides it was too hot anyway and she really wanted it moved to the dining room, where it would warm the already warm side of the house and make a lovely dinner party conversation piece. That was the next task she would undertake. Or rather the next task she would engage an expert to do for her.

The tiles of garish blue and busy green, with yellow flourishes arrived the following week and Pete bought Bob up to fix them in place.

JJ came in from the office for a new pot of coffee and noticed Bob going about his trade. "So you tile as well as dig trenches then?"

"Oh, we do a lot of things in the country. You'd be surprised."

"I am already, and impressed. You're doing a fine job Bob, which is good because those tiles are very expensive, all the way from Mudgee."

"Where?"

"Outback New South Wales"

"Oh," said Bob nonplussed. "Not a lot of call for tiling nowadays. Most folk put up plastic or tin splashboards. Some rich folk use Huon Pine, for that real country style, but there's not much of that around these days. It's mostly turned into spoons and souvenir trinkets," Bob finished with a slightly peeved tone and grouted another row of tiles.

"Well must get back to it," said JJ, filling a six cup stainless steel coffee plunger. "This should keep me going for a bit."

Bob soon fixed the last tile in place and let Gill know he'd finished and how grateful he was for the loan of the tile cutter, as his was a bit blunt. He washed up, packed away his tools, including the tile cutter, was paid in cash and away home, via the pub with Pete.

"Good day Bob, all knocked off?" Shiv welcomed him from behind the bar.

"Yep, nicely sorted. Dunno about the next job but. She said something about shifting that old stove."

"What? the old wood stove?" sparked Shiv. "That'll look nice in the shack Pete."

"It would, but the silly cow wants to shift it into the dining room."

Shiv shook his head, Bob and Pete joined him. "It'll take some lifting," he mused. "Anyone got any lifting gear?"

"Nah but there's probably a trolley or two in the shed," suggested Pete, and they roared.

❀

Having, at long last, settled on the correct arrangement of the toaster, kettle, coffee machine and blender, along the exterior and vase, napkin rings, egg basket, knife block and other peripherals, on the new island bench, Gill cast her interior designer's eye to the old black stove on its low brick pedestal.

Turning to JJ, his man bun lost after a hard day's coding, she informed him that it needed to be moved, complete with bricks, to the dining room and a new convection stove fitted in its place. "You know like we had in the old place."

JJ's draw dropped. "Can you move things like that? I thought it was kind of plumbed in, like the house was built around it. Besides I was hoping to use it for some fancy slow cooking. You know like that restaurant we used to go to. Dimploe wasn't it? The small portions, big plate and even big price place."

"But can't you do that in the dining room? It's only next door and when we have people over you can serve straight from the oven."

"No," he said emphatically, "It needs to stay in the kitchen. Besides, you said you loved its homeliness. I remember you said imagine all the family dinners lovingly cooked on that, stews and soups to warm you after a hard day in the fields."

"Yes, but I was talking about the old folk that lived here. And you're not exactly sweating in the fields baling hay."

"It's part of the house, part of the kitchen, it's that special warmth of a wood stove, that Grannie's kitchen sort of thing you love."

"I know," said Gill, with a tone of resignation. "But I don't know how to cook on it, and it needs wood, which is heavy and then there's splinters and ash and... it's just too hard." She concluded. Her resignation descending almost to a sob.

"It's country, darling," JJ said moving closer. "We came here for space and quiet. Peace of mind, a slower pace."

"But I want comfort. Can't we have both?" she pleaded.

A moment of silence followed. They both stared onto the paddock, through gleaming windows, at the wallabies cropping the remaining grass in the low sun.

"Well, you haven't slowed down, just stopped going into the office," she said with a hint of spite and a whiff of nasty.

"I know. I need to get better organised. But I can't just turn off. Supposing something goes wrong and I'm not online. How will people get what they need?"

"What they need," she retorted, spite turning to sarcasm. "It's 24 hour shopping."

"I know but it's the way of the world. Even here. I post an ad for a window cleaner, one turns up the next day. It's convenient and we love it." He paused weighing up the merit of throwing her argument back at her, not wanting to inflame things but set on keeping the stove where it was. "Like we love comfort... And it puts food on the table."

"Quicker than that thing," Gill grunted, flapping an arm in the direction of the old black stove.

The next day JJ got onto the local notice board and ordered some firewood.

The following day Dazza reversed his fuming truck up the drive and tipped out a couple of tons of heavy logs.

"You'll need to season it a couple of months, or it won't burn right," he advised, climbing down from the cab, one belly roll after another, then reaching beneath to hitch up his jeans.

"Season?" Said Gill, puzzled and stepping back a little. "Is there a season for firewood?"

"Dry it love, or it it'll clog up your flue, it's still 20 percent wet." He said counting his cash, before climbing back in the cab, flashing a dark hairy arse crack on the way.

"How do I do that?" shouted Gill.

"Stack it right, love" Dazza shouted over the top of the grumbling truck engine, and with that was off down the drive in a cloud of black diesel fumes.

Gill gathered two pieces she thought looked dry and not too heavy. She put three sheets of newspaper in the fire box, the two bits of wood, lit the newspaper and tried to close the door, which jammed on the oversized wood. She tried again, smoke billowed from the open door, before the newspaper burned out. She opened all the windows. grabbed a towel pulled out the logs and tossed them out.

JJ heard the clunk and came out of his office. "What are you trying to do? Burn the place down?"

Gill laughed. "Fat chance. I can't even light a fire and the wood doesn't fit."

JJ felt a little embarrassed, apologised and took the two ejected logs into the shed. He surveyed the wall of tools and odds and sods in front of him. Just beyond a lawnmower size gap was a work bench with vice. He managed to clamp one of the logs down then went in search of a saw. He passed by a 36 inch chainsaw, thinking it was probably not the right tool and somewhat nervous about the power of such a beast. He opened a circular saw box but found it empty, likewise a couple of other promising power tool boxes. He lifted a dust sheet to reveal a monster of a drop saw, drill press and another beast he had no idea about but looked like it made grooves in planks.

Something deep within, probably unrealised masculinity, set him in proud awe. Then he noticed a shadow board behind the power tools. There were gaps where wrenches were outlined, but he found a hand saw and soon lopped a chunk off the end of each log.

Returning to the kitchen, and channelling a virtual reality show he'd seen, where city folk learned how to light a fire, he suggested they needed some kindling. "You know, leaves and twigs," he said.

Together they went up the hill a little way and collected a basket of kindling, which lit the logs and billowed a damp grey chuff of smoke from the chimney.

"He said it would need drying first, for a couple of months, before it would burn properly," Gill related.

"Oh well it's burning now. Don't know about cutting two ton down to size though. Might see if I can get some smaller and dryer," said JJ, determined in his manoeuvre to retain the stove where it was.

"Hey, we lit a fire," Gill smiled. Then pulled a frozen pie from the freezer.

Such was her enthusiasm and sense of achievement.

Three hours later, the fire was out and pie barely defrosted.

Back on to Dazza the next day, JJ was informed, smaller could be done but there wasn't any dry wood for a month, when most folk needed it for winter and he was pretty busy delivering logs to folk that cut their own to size, and he could do logs for him if wanted that. Boldly, JJ accepted the offer of full logs and mused about the prospect of cutting wood to size, but the allure of the chainsaw in the shed had captured his manly imagination, while he thought it might be what was needed to retain the stove on its throne in the kitchen.

Saturday night rolled around. Gill levered JJ out of the office, insisting five 14 hour days was enough, while reminding him that 24 hour shopping could manage without him for a bit.

Unable to get a good cooking fire in the stove and sick of microwave meals they decided to venture down the pub. They'd discovered there were two in town, which was more than any suburb of a greater size could boast, but this was the country and JJ and Gill, were starting to realise things were different in the country.

They trundled down to the Raft. They were quite hopeful at how it billed itself as a bit of a gastro pub, which, unbeknown to both, was really one of only two choices any country pub had to stay in business. The other being pokies, which the Possum Trap, known locally as The Trap, with all the ambience of a couple of shoved together demountable classrooms, did at the other end of town.

The Raft, on the other hand, had caught Gill's eye with its double storey sandstone and weatherboard heft. A little dilapidated on three sides, it presented its best face to the street. Saturday night was curry night, courtesy of a couple of old hippies that spent some time on an ashram in the late seventies. They did vegetarian, but not vegan, as they, like most folk in town realised that growing anything without keeping animals, at least for their shit, was pushing it up hill. Besides the publicans Big and Wee Al were devout carnivores, to the extent that a meal without meat was simply a snack.

Gill had put on her best Goth black with a tasteful dash of glitter and pearls, while JJ went for skinny jeans a tight man bun and a lilac and blue checked shirt, thinking, mistakenly of course, that the checks might help him fit in with the locals a bit.

Shiv welcomed them from behind the bar, Big Al and sometimes Wee Al pretty much ran the pub with a weight of silence like a couple of mobster standover men. They gave you a nodding smile and grunt and waited for your order. JJ and Gill were happy to see a familiar face and looked at each other murmuring, "Barman as well."

"Multi skilling is the thing here then," bantered JJ.

"It's country mate. If you don't have a go at things yourself you'd sometimes be a long time waiting. Think about how the settlers managed. Couldn't pop down the shop for everything, or order online."

"I suppose," admitted JJ, knocked a tad off balance by Shiv's unwitting perception, before recovering and ordering the only fancy IPA on the shelf for himself and a glass of lightly chilled Pinot.

"Sorry mate just room temp Pinot. Only keep the whites in the fridge."

"Did you ever wonder what room temperature is? Surely it's different between here and, say Darwin. But ok," said JJ, bantering back on the front foot.

Shiv looked a bit quizzical and reached for a bottle of local Pinot Noir with a wombat on the label. "Fair point, I guess. Also depends on the time of year I suppose. When I was in the Top End it was always stinking hot. So yer room temp red would be like cold tea. Guess that's why they drink more beer."

"Cheaper by the bottle," chimed in Bob, perched on a nearby stall, oblivious to room temperature.

"True," confirmed Shiv, hovering the open bottle over a glass. "You dining here tonight?"

"Thought we might."

"You're going to need more than a glass then."

JJ agreed and Shiv stood the bottle on the bar next to the glass.

"So you've been up to the tropics then?" JJ asked Shiv.

"Couple of years back, for a season. We're not all country bumpkins you know." Then glancing to his left, "Except for Old Bob here. Born and bred in the valley. Gone forty before seeing the city."

"That was only because I busted my leg. Otherwise 64 years in the valley," Bob proudly qualified and was seconded by a small black and tan mongrel dog at his feet, that cocked its only ear in confirmation.

"Ever wanted to travel?" Asked JJ, slightly astonished, but at the same time feeling like he was in the company of local royalty.

"Nope. Got everything I need right here, good land for growing, fresh air, friends and good fishing. What more do you need?"

"So you're about as local as they come."

"S'pose so. Mum and Dad had the old farm over the back of your place, and Dad's Dad before that," said Bob proudly.

"Do you still have it?"

"Nope. Well a bit. Dad got into trouble in the sixties. The market for apples dropped right out when the Poms went into Europe. Makes you laugh now don't it? Grubbed out the orchard and ran cattle, but so did everyone, so he ended up subdividing." A hint of a scowl crept into his tone and he emptied his glass before continuing. "Put a few acres aside for family but. That's where Pete's building."

"You mean the little settlement over the hill."

"That's the one. All sold pretty quick. Problem was people, they came down to live on it. Meaning we had to find somewhere else to cut firewood."

"Took you a while to learn that, didn't it Bob?" shouted Shiv from the end of the bar.

"All's well now though. Bloody hippies." Bob sparked back, waving an empty glass, before turning back to JJ. "His folks were the first to move down. Kris and Chrissy. Nice folk, it turned out... for hippies. Some just towed caravans or old buses onto the land, left kids to run feral and grew wacky baccy. But Shiv's folks worked the land and built a proper house, and grew wacky baccy, but Shiv turned out alright..."

"In spite of all that jewellery and ink," interjected Pete, across his father's bulk, pre-empting his Dad's predictable dig.

Bob laughed, elbowed Pete in the ribs. Shiv delivered Bob's beer and JJ and Gill joined in the laughter.

"His folks make a good curry too," said Bob, bringing the conversation back.

JJ and Gill shared a dubious glance. They were used to dining at the trendiest, and supposedly best restaurants in Sydney. So they weren't expecting much more than a reasonable westernised concoction from a jar of paste, while being hopeful of more. Neither thought Bob the likely owner of a sophisticated palate.

Gill, however, had been listening intently to Bob. She was a good social listener, in the way that most men are not.

"So Bob, apart from good land, fresh air, and a bit of fishing, what has kept you here for so long?" she asked with the distanced tone of an interviewer that she'd acquired from an online communications course.

Bob was on his third beer. The ordinary standard beer from the tap. "Well the girl next door for a start. Then keeping the peace."

"You were a policeman?" she said surprised, thinking that that would have meant training in the capital and a hole in 64 years in the valley.

Bob laughed "Fencing. I put most of the fences in around here and you know what they say about good fences."

"Oh," she stifled a groan, "good neighbours."

"Yep, you name it, sheep, cattle, goats, horses. You want to keep them in the paddock, call Bob, even alpacas a few years back when they got trendy," he went on, as old men with beer in their belly tend to. "Did your place for goats. Like sheep, just a bit higher and electric for extra security. So if goats are your thing, you're set. Old Jack and Jill kept a few in their time. None escaped."

Gill mused for a bit. "We haven't really thought about animals or growing anything. Thought we might start with a dog. We didn't really have space in the city. Perhaps some chickens for eggs."

"Shame to let all that good land go to waste. There's enough petting zoos around here already..." Bob advised before trailing off with caution.

"Growing nothing," chorused Pete and Shiv, finishing Bob's gripe.

Bob shook his head, in that way that said, cheeky buggers.

Gill continued her interview. "Will the girl next door be joining us?" She asked, noticing an imbalance of women.

"No, she passed on 'bout five years ago. But in a way she's always here."

"Sorry to hear that Bob," said Gill, wishing she hadn't asked.

"It's been some time and we had a great life. The most beautiful girl in the whole valley too, Pietro and Gina's daughter, used to have the chip shop. She never left the valley either." He stared remorsefully into his beer, its foamy head flattening before concluding.

"Mind you she might still be here if she had."

"Cancer," he added belatedly.

JJ ordered another beer. The trouble with fancy beer is it always comes in tiny bottles. Shiv passed the baby bottle to JJ. "He goes on a bit, but he's right you know. More and more folk keeping pets on good farmland, growing nothing and eating crap from the supermarket, that's done hundreds of miles and goes off before you get it home," he scowled. Then added. "They know a good curry but. As long as it's not their pet cow or alpaca."

JJ poured his beer from on high getting a full foamy head. "It tastes better in a glass, less gas," he said. Thinking it might impress Shiv. Took a sip and continued. "We're not farmers though, not even much in the way of gardeners. Never really grown anything."

"So what did you move down here for?"

JJ thought for a bit, watching the head on his beer subside. "Space. Really just space and quiet."

"Imagine if everyone did that. Moved to the country and did nothing. Where would our food come from."

JJ mused a bit longer this time, while he savoured the fragrant lemon and hop aroma of his tiny beer. "So what would you suggest we do with the land?"

Shiv mused also. "Everyone around here will give you a different answer. Old Bob will tell you goats, because he fenced it for goats, and there's a good market for goat meat right now. Tastes good too. Cropping is hard work and you two don't look like you're cut out for that. A mate over the hill makes a living out of his berries, but he works hard at it, especially come harvest time. Reckons once his kids get older it'll be easier. Ready made workers and cheap. He's got five so far, all under ten. Pigs are good too."

"Oh no. Gill would never go for that," said JJ halting any further suggestions.

"Do you want to order some food?" Shiv asked, pointing to the chalkboard.

"Mum and Dad keep it pretty simple and always seasonal. Four curries, three meat, one veg, dahl, rice and chapatis."

"What do you recommend?" asked JJ, a little sceptical and attracting Gill's attention.

Shiv gave them the run down. "Starting at the top. The pork vindaloo is a bit hot. Made with local pork, from Berkshire pigs. Dark and tasty free range meat. It comes from an old Italian family up in the hills. He keeps pigs mostly for his hams and salamis, and we get any surplus. Wallaby Madras is a bit more mild. The wallabies come from Pete's place. Masses of them up there. Always in season too. We spend a couple of nights up there, culling, that's polite speak for hunting. Chicken Tika Masala, is popular. Sweet and mild and the best tasting chook for miles."

"Free range?" Asked Gill, in that animal welfare, borderline vegetarian way.

"Free range for sure, almost bloody feral," guffed Shiv.

JJ and Gill looked a bit puzzled. So Shiv clarified. "Nearly everyone around here keeps chooks for eggs. Even the weekenders. Most keep a rooster too. But when the chooks go broody and then hatch more roosters they don't know what to do with them. They used to dump them at the footy oval. So we'd round them up for curry. Now folks bring them straight to Mum and Dad. Sort of community service."

"Can you eat rooster?" Gill asked.

"Sure can. Try it," Shiv continued. "The veg curry is basically whatever is growing in the garden. That's beans, beets, celery and damn zucchini right now."

"What's wrong with zucchini?" Asked Gill.

"Nothing wrong, it just takes over. Community education again. Local council now fines people if they grow more than one plant each year. We decriminalised pot and criminalised zucchini at the same time."

"Really?" Said JJ, sucked right in.

"There are stories of zucchini's kidnapping children. Mothers parking strollers, turning their back for a minute and finding a giant zucchini in the child's place. Others have reported leaving their car windows open only to return and find it full of the buggers. They'll even follow you home."

JJ at last realised the joke. "But are you serious about one plant only?"

"That bit's true... and some of the other bits."

"I've never eaten wallaby before, so I'll have the Madras," ordered Gill, a little less sceptical than before.

"And I'm curious about these roosters, so Tika Masala for me," decided JJ.

"Find a table and it'll be with you soon. Another baby beer before you go?"

JJ and Gill found a vacant table among a dozen occupied. The chatter around them was polite and mostly generated from older couples, fifty and up. Half were well dressed and freshly scrubbed in that way older conservative people who have spent most of life in an office tend to scrub and dress for a Friday night out, even down the local. The rest more casual, probably up from the beach. They talked about gardens and fishing respectively and about getting onto those jobs around the house that always seemed to get put off in favour of fishing, or a lazy beer in the garden, followed by an afternoon snooze.

Some vaguely Indian background music, sitar and jangles, completed the soundscape and JJ and Gill relaxed into the background chatter, tuning in and tuning out, amused by snippets about the new folk in Jack and Jill's old place.

A small dumpy woman, short grey hair, jeans and an orange satin top, more Rajneesh than road gang, appeared from the kitchen bearing two bowls of curry and a dish of rice. Shiv directed her to JJ and Gill.

"Chicken Tika and a Madras." She said placing them correctly. "I'm Chrissy. Did you want chapatis as well?"

"Please," they replied in unison.

The chapatis came and they used them to polish the plates like greedy, smiling children. JJ helped Gill finish the wine, who by now was just a wee bit giggly.

"Fuck me," she said, "that was great. Bloody wallaby, what?"

JJ was similarly impressed. "The chicken was like... well chicken but not ordinary chicken. Wow."

They looked around and discovered everyone else had gone.

"Go to bed early down here," said Gill.

"Unless there's a throbbing night club along the street," joked JJ to the empty bar.

There was chatter still from out the back, along with the clanking of pans and clatter of crockery. JJ took a slightly swaying path to the bar. "Hello," he called and a tall man with full grey beard, in pink T shirt and baggy knee length shorts poked his bald head round the corner.

"Yes mate?"

"Is it closing time?"

"Nope folk down here tend to bed early," he said, the remnants of a Northern English accent still evident. "They're either old and tired, been out in the sun all day, or have to get up early for animals. Mostly the first two nowadays. I'm Kris by the way. chief cook and spice grinder." He did his best to dry a dank hand and extended it. "You must be the fellow in Jack and Jill's old place."

"Yes John-Jack, JJ," he beckoned his wife over. "This is Gillianna."

"Oh Gill-with-a-G. We've heard a lot about you."

"You're the cook," assumed Gill.

"For my sins, aye. Hope it met with expectations."

"Way beyond." They began their effusive compliments.

"It's all down to quality raw ingredients. We grow the herbs and spices and folk in the hills supply the meat and veg. It's a karmic community thing," said Kris without missing a beat, or sounding too hippy like. "Tell you what, give us five minutes and we'll be done out back. We usually sit down for a nightcap then, while the boys do their thing."

JJ and Gill returned to their table. Shortly Kris and Chrissy joined them with an unmarked bottle of pale green liquid and four small glasses.

"So you bought Jack and Jill's old place," Chrissy started. "Such a lovely house and they built it all themselves. Did you know that? Dug the footings, collected the stones, mostly from their block and even milled the timber.

Lovely people too. Kind of first of the new settlers in a way. You know, like artists, or as Kris says earthworms, making nice things and goodness out of what others leave behind."

JJ soon engaged Kris on the subject of firewood. He figured that if he could get good wood, he had more chance of keeping the stove. Besides firewood seemed like a manly topic. Kris was happy to oblige, also being of the opinion that both fire and wood were men's domains.

"Dirty Dazza 's not the man to get firewood from. He'd sell you anything to get cash for pokies. He's probably up the Trap right now. I'll drop a bit up to you. Enough to get you started. You know you've got plenty up the back of your place. Jack used to cut seven or eight ton a year. Then him and Jill would plant twenty new trees. Like clockwork, three to one pretty much."

Kris poured four glasses of sweet green spirit and continued, "He used to come down hill with his trailer behind his old Fergy loaded full. They'd unload it then back up again. It's probably still up there. You'd have seen it when you looked at the place." He raised his glass looked direct at JJ, who followed suit. "You did go up hill?"

JJ looked a bit sheepish. "Actually no," he said, through intense liquorice fumes, realising then that he should have walked the land more. "We really only looked at the house and garden. Gill loved them at first sight."

Kris hid his incredulity. "You're in for a treat then. It's beautiful up there. The bush is quite different. All tall trees and big wallabies."

"And eagles," he added, as an afterthought picturing the view in his mind's eye. "You can see right down the valley to the bay and out to the mountains the other way."

Chrissy was also in full flow. She usually was after curry night and even more so with new folk to listen to her. "How are you settling in then? Not too much of a shock from... Sydney is it?" She guessed.

Gill had to pick her moment to get in or Chrissy would rattle on for another half hour and relate the entire town history. Well at least from the last 40 years.

"Yes Sydney, Paddington to be exact. Do you know it?"

"Not really. Only ever passed through places till we landed here. And passed through too many places to get to know any of them really."

"So you travelled a lot."

"Oh good lord yes. But then we landed here and found nirvana. Never left. It simply draws you in and holds you tight." She grasped Gill's hand in both of hers. "You'll see love. Now how have you found the house and what do you plan to grow? I understand Shiv and Pete have done some work for you."

Again Gill picked her entry with perfection. A skill she'd also learned from her online course and refined selling tat to inner city interior design darlings.

"Yes Shiv and Pete have done a fine job in the kitchen. I've had them take out the ugly old sink and benches and put in a nice island bench and old Bob has done a fine job with some bespoke tiles I had made. I would have never thought it would go so well."

"He likes tiles, does Bob. It's his creative side. You should see his bathroom mosaic and the one on his back veranda."

"Really?" said Gill astonished.

"Oh yes, there's more to Bob than digging holes and filling them in. He's quite the artist. So it sounds like you have the house sorted. At least the kitchen."

"Almost. I just need to get that old stove out." She said, turning to JJ with one of those, "don't we" glances, who was still talking firewood with Kris. At which point a hush fell across the table.

"You mean the old wood stove," whispered Kris.

"The black one on the bricks," breathed Chrissy.

JJ and Gill looked questioningly at each other. Then JJ said, "Well yes, but I kind of like it where it is. It seems like it was made for the place and everything else fitted around it."

"Indeed so," said Kris sternly, who seemed to speak with stern considered authority on most things.

"Ooh you don't want to go disturbing that," added Chrissy with a tone of foreboding.

"Why not?" Gill rushed in, feeling momentum was building against her. "I don't know how to cook on it anyway and it would look good in the dining room, and there's no heating in there."

Kris and Chrissy began to explain, passion and emotion eventually outriding considered authority.

"Oh no, the hearth is the soul of the house. It's where the spirits of those that lived there before, those that set the first stone and split the first shingle live. It's where the very spirits of the stones and trees that are the house live."

"Besides, who puts a stove in dining room?" interjected Kris.

"Let it speak to you and you will learn," continued Chrissy. "There's probably lots of things you don't know now, but if you let it be and remember what you first liked about the place, you will grow into it."

"I suppose, but it's hard and it all seemed like it was going to be so easy," said Gill, a little defeated.

"Think of it like this," spoke the considered tone of Kris, "you have a lovely little farm, on the edge of the village, that set you dreaming of an idyllic way of life. You can walk to the pub and walk past fields of things growing in the open. When you get home, there will be more things growing along with the warmth of a wood fire, to bake fresh bread in. You know nothing breathes homeliness like the aroma of fresh baked bread."

"And nothing nourishes the soul of the house like contented spirits, fulfilled dreams and a welcoming hearth," concluded Chrissy. "Anyway, here's to you both," she said, sensing some tension between the new arrivals and together they raised their glasses of herbal spirit. "Let's hope you find the right thing and a path that makes you happy and content in our little valley."

Walking home that night in a fog of IPA, local Pinot Noir, and whatever Kris and Chrissy plied them with, JJ and Gill passed front yards of trellised tomatoes, beans reaching up pyramid cane structures, heavy drooping vines and single zucchini plants. Then fields of sheep and cattle, goats and alpacas, potatoes, peas, onions and strawberries. A couple of small wallabies skipped across the road in front of them. A little further along, a small wallaby that hadn't made it across the road, bled scarlet on the bitumen in the half light.

They both thought of the waste. Then Gill thought of her curry.

The front of their little house, unlike most, was set back from the road, with a wide garden of flowers and herbs that spilled into each other and strayed further into the paddock and then crawled up behind the house. It shone beneath the glow of the waxing moon.

"Did you leave a light on?" JJ asked.

Gill replied in the negative. They paused at the gate. Scanned for movement.

"Look it's the moon. It's as if it's floodlit the house. Isn't it lovely?" observed Gill.

They stood at the gate some time, taking in the scent of the garden and flowering gums that drifted down the hill behind the house. Then Gill turned to JJ. "You can keep the stove. We can learn to use it. Besides they seem like nice spirits."

JJ replied, "And I think I'd like to spend less time in the office. Perhaps move my work out altogether. Perhaps learn to be more country. You know do things country for ourselves more."

She squeezed him tight. "Sounds like a plan honey."

❀

JJ bounced out of bed the next morning like a kid on Christmas Day. He patrolled the paddock beyond the garden with menace, inspecting fences posts, leaning on corner posts with intent and flexing wire. After some time he worked out the gate latch into the next paddock and dragged the gate open, then continued his inspection.

Returning, he went straight to the shed and proceeded to examine the remaining tools and equipment. He forced down the drop saw, heaved the chainsaw off the high shelf and swung it around, trying in out for size. Then with a calm resolve attempted to start it. He failed three times before checking the fuel and finding it empty. Found a green container marked "Chainsaw 2 Stroke", filled the machine, and pulled the cord. Still no go.

Then thought to do a bit of research.

Typing *Chainsaw use* into the search bar on his phone he was soon viewing one of many *YouTube* tutorials, then another, and then one with the exact same machine he had at his feet and thankfully an Australian voice. Choke, start, close choke, start, he repeated to himself. Popped his phone on the bench, exacted the mantra and the saw kicked to life. He stood back, the saw vibrated a jitterbug on the concrete floor. He grabbed it from behind, revved the trigger and felt the power, a certain traditional masculine power forever generated from internal combustion engines. "We can fucking do this." He revved the machine a few more times before pushing the off button.

Gill stood at the threshold of the back door, wrapped in silk dressing gown.

"What the …?"

"Chainsaw." He waved the now silent machine at her, trying not to look too threatening. "We can do this. We can cut our own firewood. I've got some logs coming, and we can keep some sheep and cows in the paddock and fill the freezer, and we need some chooks and there's a load of hives in the shed and... we have to get a bit dirty, but we can do this and have it all... well, what we need."

Gill smiled. "Okay. And a dog."

"And a dog," JJ agreed and they went inside for coffee and JJ, still hyped, phoned Dazza to find out when the logs would arrive. A weary and still bed fuzzed Dazza, promised delivery that arvo or the next day.

"The fences are bit saggy and there's one big hole that we'll need to fix, but there's some wire in the shed and some pliers." He sipped at his coffee, that he really didn't need, and, continued, "I'll get started on that after this while we wait for the wood and with luck we can cook on the stove tonight." He leaned back in his chair content. Gill smiled her okay smile again.

In the arvo, when JJ had finished fiddling with the chainsaw, and nicked his thumb testing and hoping it was sharp enough, which it obviously was, he set about repairing the leaky fence in the paddock. Once more he'd made use of that famous educational network and become confused from too much information, then gone back to the beginning. Spade in hand he determined to put a new bracing post in.

He was on his knees, scraping biscuits of yellow clay from a deepish hole when Kris clanked up the drive with a ute load of firewood.

"Finding your way," said Kris, loping across the paddock, hemp jeans, thongs and vaguely Bali purple T shirt. "I bought you some firewood and some of that itsy bitsy beer you like."

JJ was caught a bit off balance, when he realised his bum was in the air and his head in a hole. "G'day Kris," he said, over loudly, in an attempt to recover his blokey poise and be country. He stood brushed off his well-known bush walking brand pants and hands at the same time.

"You look like a beer would fit right now," Kris twisted two tops off and carefully placed the caps in his pocket. JJ took one and they swallowed half a bottle each in unison. "It's not bad beer really," Kris said, "it's just the puny bottles it comes in."

They swallowed the remains. "You might be right," admitted JJ.

"Jack was always meaning to do this fence. It was one of those things. I think he kept it as a to do job, just so he had a to do job to do. Something to keep him from reaching the end." Kris peered into the hole. "Find anything interesting in there?"

"Dirt and rocks and now clay" the two men sat down around the hole and made inroads into another beer.

"I get the feeling there's a big difference between the hills and the valley," JJ said, glancing past the fence upward to the treelined brow, where he guessed his property ended.

Kris rolled a joint, after ascertaining with a glance and receiving a nod in reply that it was ok, lit it, took a slight draw and passed it on. "You mean more than geography?" JJ took a drag and passed the joint back, Kris took another drag and continued in that authoritative tone that Chrissy usually moderated. "Folk are not that different really. It's just they can't see what they have in common."

JJ took another drag, coughed a little and passed the joint back to a beckoning Kris, who went on as bush philosophers with a joint in their hand tend to. "The valley folk don't really like the hill folk because the hill folk don't spend and they don't spend because they don't work in the way the valley folk think they should. While the hill folk don't want to work or spend or be part of that whole cycle, at least not as the main plank to their way of life.

"It's like this. Valley folk keep big paddocks for big animals and live in big houses that they pay for most of their lives so have to keep doing that work thing.

"The hill folk, on the other hand, have no paddocks, well they have a few corrals and sheds but by and large no fences and eat small animals and live in small houses that they add to if and when needed and have no debt so don't need that work thing."

JJ gestured he was following. Kris kept going. "The valley folk don't understand how the hill folk live, how they can rely on small animals and not want a freezer full of beef."

JJ sipped at his puny beer. "How do they?"

"They trap and hunt and keep the land so it attracts the wallaby. Which the valley folk don't like because when they come down from the hills they eat the grass in their paddocks. You see beyond the hills is a rich larder. In the Lost West the animals are protected and the hill folk know that, so they, in turn, protect the wilderness. It's sort of an integrated thing.

"But the valley folk can't live without the security of a freezer full of beef and butchers and a slaughter yard." Kris paused sipping his beer, to make it last, then roared, "They'd all be vegetarian if they had to get their own meat."

JJ laughed and beckoned the joint back, which Kris had a habit of sitting on.

"But there are things you need, to build and cook and hunt and trap and you'd have to grow some veg, surely?"

"Yeh, veg is mostly in cages and a bit of hydroponic growing. You're right though, hammers, nails, saws, fuel, and basics, flour, sugar tea: station rations. That's when the hill folk come to the valley, but the valley folk, especially Ancy, reckons they should spend more with him and buy shit they don't need."

JJ partially reclined on one elbow. "So apart from one-off tools it's fuel and food."

"Yeh, bog roll and soap, too. I always forget that, women are pretty keen on bog roll, there's a few make soap up there and trade it, but bog roll is a must. No one makes their own dunny paper."

"I suppose we all shit."

"Yep and eat. It's food that brings people together. It's kind of what we do at the pub on Friday night. Everyone loves a good curry and the valley folk get a bit of exotica with a wallaby or rooster curry, and the occasional hill folk that venture down for special occasions, which they do. Usually big birthdays, you know fifty, sixty, sometimes twenty-one, but they usually have a big bash in the bush. Anniversaries are oddly popular. Not many get married up there, but they always remember the first time they went to bed together, or roughly when.

"There's not much other choice really except the chippy, which is good, does a nice pizza too, but it's not really special occasion stuff and there's really nowhere for a sit down meal, which makes a change from a barbie in the back yard." Kris trailed off trying to regather the thread. "So yeh they get to taste beef or lamb. It's all about eating, and like you say shitting. If folk could see that we'd all be better off."

JJ stirred from a haze he'd unwittingly slumbered in to. "So you and Chrissy kind of live in both worlds. You have the best of both dipping in and out."

"Sort of. We live more in the hills than valley though." Kris thought for a bit. "Yeh, we wouldn't be here if we didn't have our place in the hills. It's our haven, as Chrissy says, our piece of nirvana. It's about keeping the ordinary greedy work, the stuff that stresses you out, at arm's length. You still talk to folk but you don't invite them home. We're not like some folk though with big gates and big dogs and big fuck off signs. We don't mind visitors, but once you come up our drive it's our world with different rules.

"Which I suppose is the same as the big gates, dogs and fuck off signs. Its folks setting their own rules, just some are a bit more out there than others. I expect you got yours, but I don't expect I'll see any vicious black dogs in the drive."

"Or fuck off signs." JJ sat up to receive the last of the six tiny beers. "Yeh we have to get sorted, make a few changes." He savoured his beer, as you do the last of most things. "We really don't know what we're doing." He dropped back onto his elbow. "Gill loves the place. She always wanted to live in the country, and I could see that city life was getting to us both. She had a bit of money come her way from a maiden aunt, and we were really over our place in town, so we took the plunge. Between what we got for our place and Gill's inheritance, we have no debt now. It's bloody great. You know, not wondering if you can pay the mortgage every month." He had more to say but paused thoughtfully. "The problem is I can't stop working. I don't know how I'd fill my day if I didn't."

"You're in the country now. Not just the country but Hidden Valley. It's different here. You have to learn to set your own pace, fill your time in your own way." Kris was recovering from his own smoke induced malaise and back into authoritative mode. "You have to recognise that what you do for yourself here, to keep yourself warm, provide food and care for animals is worth much more than cash in the bank. If you can learn to do those things, you sleep well and live well and your spirit will be in good health."

JJ nodded in agreement, without being convinced. "How did you do it. You know unshackle from work, take control?"

"You mean take control of that work ethic you get indoctrinated with through school, parents, TV, and in everything you see and hear?" Kris was on a roll now. Chrissy would have tripped him just as he was stepping up to the soapbox. "It's everywhere. Even so-called rebel music. It's all bullshit, it's all about giving praise to the working man and woman. And it's all about feeding the value of money and look at the greed it developed. People don't know how to thrive anymore. They've lost sight of what it is to live well and think more. To them more and more shit is the answer and they don't give a shit about the mess they leave." Kris paused looked disgusted at his almost empty bottle before ranting on.

"There's good folk in the hills and scum, and there's the same in the valley, but there's a lot of useless twats too. You know the ones that think they're doing the right thing but are still hooked on brand names, but ethical brand names, like ethical food. They're still shopping, still consuming and couldn't feed themselves if the freight couldn't get over the mountain and the power went down." He paused for breath and emptied the last dregs from the bottle. "And they're still propping up the system with their investments and superfunds when it comes to the bottom line. Look at them all along the waterfront." Kris paused again, gathering his pouch. "But they like a good curry too." He laughed, mostly at his own diatribe and its end. "I'd best be off before I get carried away."

JJ stood with Kris. "No worries and thanks. Thanks for the firewood too. The stove is staying by the way."

"Pleased to hear that. Chrissy will be pleased. Don't know why you'd want to move it to the other room anyway."

"No, me neither. It's kind of how Gill thinks. Moving stuff around. It engages her."

"You'll find your way mate."

They tipped the empty bottles into the recycling bin behind the house, unloaded the wood and Kris poked his head into the kitchen to say goodbye to Gill, who thrust a hot jar into his hand.

"Pears," She said with the pride of a new mum, "there's heaps on the tree out the front," then returned to the kitchen island, now cleared of frills and populated with a chopping board and knife, a bucket of pears, a big bowl and a dozen or so preserving jars. On the stove was a massive pot emitting stream. "And I found boxes of these jars in the shed and a recipe online. It's easy, just pears and sugar." She confirmed that with her phone propped against the knife block. Stood back to admire the stove, the kitchen island and six already processed gleaming jars at the window.

"Proper country cottage, love."

"Yes darling, that's all you need, it's simple."

"Finding your way both. See you again," Kris said leaving with a bounce in his step born of new found friends.

❁

It took JJ the best part of a week to set a new post in place and patch up the fence in a sort of abstract pattern of intersecting wire, approximating the mesh that had been there. With thoughts of pure bred and exotic livestock to fill the paddock on his mind, JJ fired up the coffee machine when above the choking sound of the espresso beast he heard a crash like a falling tree, then the clang of metal and another crash, followed by an extremely painful kind and squeal like a bleat he couldn't place and the silence of his coffee machine.

Rushing to the front door he discovered the carnage was some way up the road. One power pole down, along with the nearby fence, another fence further along the road smashed, a truck in the ditch and logs spewed across the road.

"Fuck," he said for the second time in a day and called Gill from the lounge, where she was looking at very expensive invented breed designer dogs. She repeated JJ's exclamation.

A blubber of a man extricated himself in stages from the ditch parked truck, just as a herd of young Highland Cattle began to make their way through the new hole carved in the fence. Dazza attempted to clamber back in the cab of his prone truck, but the angle was too steep to haul his lard and the hairy cows quickly engulfed his retreating hairy arse.

From further along the road, Gill thought she saw sheep leaping across ditches, she fled indoors dragging JJ with her as the cattle ventured up their drive, through the garden and into the paddock, through the gate JJ had forgotten to close. There they browsed for a moment before crashing through the patched up fence, JJ had spent the morning attending to, with the ease of, well, a log laden truck crashing through a wire fence.

Gill called the local nursing centre to report the accident. Carol had furnished her with all the important numbers on a fridge magnet, that sat alongside Dazza's. They asked if there were any other vehicles. Gill went to the front door, peeked through the window, and jolted back, dropping the phone, startled by a split lipped mohawk monster licking her window. She picked up the phone. "No but there are animals everywhere."

By Sunday lunchtime the Whistlebrows, like most other weekenders, had left for the city, so there was little activity in neighbouring properties, and JJ and Gill weren't game to venture out when the ambulance arrived, along with the nurse on duty. An officious and effective older women with a

Germanic disposition and accent, and the volunteer driver, Doc Dory plopped out steadying herself on her stick. The nurse made her way to the truck in the ditch. As she did, a dazed Dazza, crawled out from beneath. The look on Doc Dory's face spoke a thousand expletives. Then the volunteer fire brigade arrived, along with the local plod. The fire brigade belly laughed to a man and woman. They all bar one had plentiful bellies to laugh with, while Constable Boggo realised someone needed to be responsible and arranged for the road to be cleared, and breath tested the sheepish Dazza, who professed his innocence, pointing to the somewhat splattered and spread limbs of an alpaca he had failed to avoid.

At the sight of the authorities taking control of the situation, JJ and Gill ventured along the road. They explained there were lots of animals heading up the hill through their place and that the logs on the road were to be delivered to their place, over a week ago.

"Well," said the young slim, apparent leader of the volunteer fire brigade, pushing his oversize helmet back, "well Gill-with-a-G, I suppose we could dump them up there for you."

Gill smiled another ok smile and said, "Thanks Pete, that would be nice."

"What about the animals?" JJ asked.

"Not a lot we can do about them."

"They're gone," corroborated another firey from beneath a big plastic hat.

"Don't think we are going to try and round them up in the bush," continued Pete. The other members of the crew shuffled and muttered in agreement, stifling sniggers. "Help yourself though if you like. Good meat."

The logs were duly dumped in the paddock next to the house. JJ set about them, tentatively, following a couple more video tutorials. In the days that followed, Bob came round to show JJ how to fix the fence and Gill dragged the hives out of the shed and Chrissy put her in touch with a place to get bees.

A couple of weeks later Shiv and Pete popped round with a whole cow for the freezer and at the local market on the weekend Gill bought a couple of lovely Highland Cattle and Alpaca skin rugs from a freshly perfumed Flathead to set the lounge off just right. The stove worked brilliantly, not just cooking bread and Sunday roasts but also providing that special country ambience that the glossy photographs in magazines just can't convey. Down at the pub beef Madras was on special.

The Whistlebrows and the Albrights with the alpacas did wonder about the empty paddocks and made an enquiry at the local cop shop, but were simply told there was an accident as a result of an animal escaping and that those in the accident didn't feel the need to take it any further, but they should make sure their animals were kept under control. The Whistlebrows and Albrights, apologised for the inconvenience and treated themselves to a nice meal at the pub where they met Bob and, wanting to be good neighbours, engaged him to fix the fences.

Just as winter set properly in with a couple of harsh fingertip nipping frosts, enough to get most of the waterfront locking up, or in the case of the Furphys, flicking the switch to bring down the shutters, and fleeing north, Clancy finally got inside the CWA HQ to address the ladies at a sewing bee.

He badgered his sister Mavis, Mavis Reeves that is, into submission, claiming to want to know what the ladies wanted. Simo Reeves knew too well to hold his tongue when brother and sister were in heated discussion. He had grown to know Clancy too well from schooldays when the two of them and Bob were the only boys of the same age in class and expected to be friends. The three of them got on only because they all had younger sisters.

Clancy and Simo traded sisters, and Bob's sister got out first chance she got.

The butcher's wife disliked her brother in a way that little sisters dislike bullying big brothers, but rather than letting him know with a lashing tongue as sharp as her husband's knife, she pasted on a smile as obsequious as Clancy's. If the two had got really close, too close for brother and sister, their smarm would have melted into one common pool of the slimiest DNA.

At the meeting Mavis showed her brother the quilt she and the other ladies were working on. It illustrated the founding of Shipwreck, including an embroidered representation of the raft, featuring survivors reaching out for the shore, a remarkable likeness of her husband leading the way.

Well, Clancy's skin grew tight, and turned the colour of one Reeves's sausages, made from mangled mutton, drenched in beef flavouring and colouring in a hot pan full of fat. Mavis asked Clancy what he thought and if he'd like to contribute to the quilt. Clancy just about contained himself when Gracie McGrath, whose likeness seemed to be supporting Sleepy Reeves reach for land, offered him a needle and thread which he snatched at and that was that.

❀

Now it is tempting to close this story with a big bang and a splattering of guts and other goop all over the time bleached floral wallpaper but it's a more truthful account that Clancy fell to the floor twitching, crippled by a stroke.

"Well," huffed Mavis, "never happy that man. I suppose someone should call the ambulance."

A gaggle of elderly and mostly flabby women shuffled through their bags, fumbling for the mobile phones their children had insisted they carry at all times.

"Does anyone know how to use these things?" Asked Gracie McGrath, pressing five buttons at once with two bony fingers.

Then May McDo dropped her phone and it bounced off poor old Clancy's head, which was almost still by now. Mary McDo was the voice of reason, as she had been among the CWA for many years. "He's a mean ugly bastard but we'd best do the right thing."

❀

It was some time before Clancy returned to Shipwreck, barely able to speak, rarely out of a wheelchair and at the whim of the woman he'd bullied for years. His diet was bread and water, or rather bread in water, that he could just about scoop up with a cramped claw. The same one he used to drive his wheelchair via a little knob that he seemed to always have his hand on, usually at people but always missing.

His return to Shipwreck was indeed timely, for while he'd been rendered almost mute, his facility for speech reduced two dribbled words "Ancy" and what sounded like an attempt to curse but ended up a spray of saliva, he had also gained a seat on the local council, thanks largely to a swag of votes from new blowins, naive to his reputation. As his primary carer Mavis made sure he took up his seat and lifted his claw to vote, or not.

# Chapter 4

## Misfortune: A New Beginning

The winter after the highlanders escaped to their natural habitat and the folk that visited The Raft on a Saturday night acquired a taste for Beef Madras, was a kind winter. Even the western banshees came with soft lilt, bringing with them generous showers. The creeks ran fast, but not too fast and in between were crystal days of clarity, from half past noon to half past three.

The mountain folk wallowed in the darkness that, to them, felt like a holiday, a six or seven month long holiday. For most it was seen as time to repair, to recover bodies and sometimes minds that had become stretched over the heated summer, mostly in preparation for the expected malevolent gales of spring that failed to eventuate. Wood piles remained three fence posts long when spring suggested an end to the flimsy frosts that set in the vegie patches, glossing the kale and beet, the standard winter fodder for people and beasts.

In the valley a similar tale was emerging. Those that stayed through winter wrote glowingly to friends and relatives far away about the brilliance of the winter sun, albeit fleeting, and of a year when the livestock loss was minimal. Weekenders spent more weekends in the valley. Two weekers spent long weekends as well. Most embracing the notion of ye olde log fire in ye olde country cottage. Probably also, like the mountain folk, wanting to spend more time with their Alpaca and Highland Cow rugs that they'd installed during the autumn.

Likewise downtown and along the Esplanade, while it wasn't quite so effusive, dank fog most of the day rarely is, in particular the heavy ones that crawl down any gap at the back of your neck and from there seep, chillingly, into your spine and shudder through your core. But other than those days, they also texted and emailed of the great life to be had in Hidden Valley.

It got to the point that real estate was not advertised in the normal way, which preserved the beauty of most roads. Instead it changed hands through word of mouth, and the usual bourgeois clubs and networks. As a result, the population of Hidden Valley grew tenfold, to a hundred times that of those that blew in on the crude raft almost two centuries ago.

As spring broke the dark, growth was luxuriant. People could be seen throughout the Valley turning compost, spreading mulch, only the new, naive folk, or Coboldis tilled anymore. The Coboldis were, however, always forgiven for their contribution to the carbon escaping, simply because their pork was considered the finest for hills and valleys around, especially the bacon Reeves made from the middles, and even more so since Faffy Floyd had relocated to The Valley and made a TV show out of pretending he was the first to set sight on Hidden Valley in decades and discover how wonderful it was and tell the locals how to do things while he was at it.

Faf had bought the old Berger farm for a song, after Clancy's stroke meant they had to move closer to care. Unlike most blowins, Faf, Fleur, and two urchins that hadn't discovered or developed any identity, other than the name allotted them from the lame imagination or tradition of family, were young with shitloads of energy. Like mountain folk, without the drugs, hang ups, syndromes, or as many children and definitely not as many former partners—a mild winter means folk tend wander more than usual.

No, the Floyds breezed in, with their corporate tarnish and lifestyle styling, like they were exhaled from another planet. The great formalisers that gave value to the folk of the high country, the folk who chose to live beneath the breath of the Lost West.

There was, however, much latitudinal strife. The town folk suspicious of the bundles of crops hill folk brought to market each month. Weekenders mostly oblivious. And as the gardens gave and grew, so the bush grew lush.

Padichew, became the most popular snack, macerated by both children and adults. A dried meat of small wallaby, made salty and sweet and intoxicatingly umami, it bore the face of Faf on its wrappers and made him more popular than the former resident of his recently rechristened farm "Big Bullocks", could ever have been.

❋

It was as everything seemed to be bobbing along swimmingly, blowins ecstatic, locals cashed up and mountain folk with early crops and burgeoning gardens, that the serene summer sky, spat lightening into the Lost West and smote Hidden Valley of its joy. Or whatever deities of ancient myths and legends do to ordinary folk that are just enjoying themselves. Fleeing from their homes under threat of inferno or choking smoke they took to the river's edge

Every evening, while seeking refuge at the river, unknowing of their homes' survival, a bean pole of a man would speak in an ancient tongue. He called it poetry, others called it spoken word, some called an oration and yet others called it an atrocity and pulled their gobsmacked children away, hurrying them back to tents and vans, ushering their attention back to small sticky screens

Shaded beneath a canvas hat that hung and swivelled like a lampshade and hid most of his face except for a fungused chin that, over the last couple of weeks, since his wife Kathy had been away, seemed to be growing oyster mushrooms around the cavernous mouth that issued a summary of the current state of affairs, but otherwise horrified with its unlighted vacuum.

Robo never liked his dentures and found it easier to report his daily circuit of the fire front without fear of them dropping out.

Robo's home was the furthest into the mountains, along a steep wooded spur that climbed into the hills of Bloodbury. So high and remote was his home that the springs that filled the river below lay within his land and the springs fed the homestead that was bountiful in meat and vegetable and berries and cheese and most of what they needed. Yet for all that, Robo's touch was light and he perched on the land, staking his claim with tender claw.

Beneath a solitary oak, formerly alone on the Esplanade, now arced on three sides by various makeshift shelters, Robo would begin his report, a bellowing gust crashing from the chasm and fluttering the frill of his flabby beard, as he cried his verse.

### To The River

*It was a day*
*a day of becoming,*
*a day of regret.*
*When highlanders*
*and folk of the slopes*
*fled to the river.*

*Along the shores*
*of the estuarine refuge*
*camped the hill folk*
*and those that sought*
*the peace of the valley's end.*

*Along the bank*
*they set out their jewels,*
*their loved ones*
*and keepsakes.*

In the evening
they sat helpless.
The scientists talking
of data and goals.
The poets speaking
of imagery and language.
The sailor discusses
the light and tide
and the farmer
the lack of rain.

Together we spoke of home,
love and whisky.
It's language widely known
it's meaning less easy.

The long beard and his woman
in equally long skirt,
move uncomfortably
among the inebriated.
Home schooled children
boggle eyed.
Those of an uncomfortable fit,
those that turned their back
and sought the solace of the land.
Those that have grown of the land
and into the land.

Along the river's edge
they meld with workaday denizens,
retiring tree changers,
their fit as awkward.

But those of the hills
and those of the river,
fisherfolk, sailors,
builders of boats,
smallholders,
small farmers.
We share a common thread
of strength
of stoic activity.

Indeed such was the activity that a small village of refugees, in a hodgepodge of canopies, strung from vehicles and trees, mushroomed, like the growth of Robo's chin, overnight, growing in ever increasing rainbows.

**The Camp**

To the water's edge
we flock
in search of safe harbour,
like thousands before.
Strangers unknown, unwanted,
dislocated, displaced.
First world refugees.
We pitch our tents park our vans,

tether our goats
and corral our sheep.
Unroll our swags
on cold steel flat trays,
Kelpies by our side and hope.
Hope we will have a home to return to.

At the end of the second day Robo's oratory was preceded by a loose ensemble of strings plucked and bowed and pipes blown with sweet distraction and defiance. Distraction from the plume overhead and defiance of petty officialdom.

## Maggot

As with the millions elsewhere,
dislocated and displaced
in search of refuge,
an egregious official patrols the camp.

Fat man on a bicycle,
humanity's corrupt umpire.
Absent of empathy.
Resplendent in his inflated power,
and shiny badge.

"You can't camp here. Move along."
He bellows
like a preacher
against the backdrop of hell's fury
rising from the west.

Helicopters overhead,
dredge the bay
filling water bombs
then labour back
into the darkening sky.

In shock we turned,
then turned away
as if a foreign language spoken.

We tend our stock
busting open hay bales
cutting riverside sedge
replenishing troughs.
Dismissing the fat man.
As one would a fool with no sense
of time,
of place,
of people,
of emergency raging
just ten minutes away.
So we stay busy in search of normality.

With persistence
outdoing common sense,
like most petty officials
with petty badges
and little authority,

he seeks to impose himself
and as if by osmosis
his message is heard.

With anger born
of absurdity
his gaze is drawn to the sky.
The situation spelt out
Like an angry texter
In thumping block capitals
FIRE
E ...M E R... G E N C Y

"You can't camp here." He persists.
"Move along."
He orders.
"Get a brain." He is told.
"I've got one." He replies.
"Then use it
to find your heart."

And so the rage
in the bush
and on the foreshore continues.
Until the latter
is waved away.
After noting
names and numbers with a promise
to take matters further.

*Remounting his cycle*
*he puffs away,*
*with each push*
*of a complaining pedal,*
*to refrains of anatomical doubt.*

It is a fact that the band that tripped and chugged its way through various standards and banjo driven dances came to coalesce out of anger. Not at the fire that choked their lungs and threatened their homes, but out of a determination to stay, and long beards, ferals, circus folk and blowins and every displaced person with half a gift, knack or talent came to offer relief through some form of entertainment.

Soon children of farmers and grandchildren of blowins were queuing up to play with straggle haired, unwashed urchins, learning to walk a slack rope, juggling or tumbling into the half light of late night. A line was drawn however when a well-dressed twelve year old sought to learn sword swallowing and both dread headed, would-be mentor, and lifestyle coach grandmother convinced the young waif that it would make an honourable long term career goal.

The festival atmosphere lingered beyond the fall of the sun, into the early morning, songs sung in circles the centre absent of the typical campfire for obvious reasons. Bottles of ale, and wine, spirits of many colours passed around till falling down the circle was broken.

## Sleep

*There was little comfort.*
*The lapping tide*
*and freeway traffic*
*both unfamiliar to many.*

Animals used to night barns
complained in chorus,
tethered to fences.
Sleep and anxiety
and the unknown
blend so badly
that goats used to bleating for milking
were woken
by their owners.

Eventually anxiety saw off sleep.
Radios clicked and tuned in
to scratchy AM reports.
Mobile phone screens
illuminated the thinly veiled privacy
of tents and caravans.

Kettles wheezed
and coffee pots coughed.
Along the main road a convoy of red
and with each gulp
a growing sense of dread.

Robo was always the first soul to wander the camp. The first witness to day's light. Light that loomed grey barely seemed to leave. His heavy boots plodded through the tangle of tents, as large and small figures groaned and stretched to life. Then wrapping themselves in clothes at hand stood to view the encroaching smoke.

## Hope

Soon anxiousness and dread
turned to inquiry and hope
and a way home was sought.
For while the means to shift some animals existed,
others had to be left.
stalls open, gates ajar,
to fend for themselves.
So with hope
and strength
they approached the roadblock
that marked the southern edge.
Young girls in cadet uniforms
brandishing cake
questioned
"Are you going to defend your home?"
And given an emphatic yes
they continued their breakfast.

The air grew thicker,
vision more difficult
with each minute west.

Essential Access Only
read the hastily propped sign.

Slowly they drove
as the valley grew narrow.

*In a strange inertia*
*of wanting to know*
*but knowing*
*the longer they didn't*
*the longer their home would stand.*
*They counted houses and examined*
*the gardens and hills as never before.*

*Green lines*
*at each driveway indicated,*
*they guessed, those evacuated.*
*Hope grew bold with each green line*
*and each green hill.*
*As they rounded*
*the last bend,*
*chickens scattered*
*across the road*
*and ignoring the white rooster*
*that raced within a whisker*
*they spied*
*their home*
*untouched.*

At the conclusion of that third oration a mighty cheer resounded. A bold sense of survival, of resilience, spread through the camp. No home lost, or life threatened. Reports from the front lines around the valley leavened bravado into optimism.

The following morning Robo went with a couple of older women, uncertain of their ability to inspect their home which

lay in The Glen, in direct line of the fire and on return to camp
that evening his report carried more a tone of caution and
foreboding

## Pink Ribbons

Along the rivulet and valley slopes rest houses
of stick and plank and iron roofs.
A timber cutter's cottage,
old schoolhouse, pickers' huts and hermitage
of a hundred years or more.


Their myriad gables poking through gardens almost as old.
Now pink ribbon garnished.
Indefensible,
their heritage submitted to the flame
to the roar
that ravages the hills
not two drop punts away.


Owners stand bereft,
the thought of loss
numbing.


Stilled moments beneath the heat
and embers
that fall as leaves
and bark
from the blackened sky.

Holding back tears

that will not quench a flame

churning stomachs

that will not dampen a coal

they reach for towels

hoses and woollen rugs.

Gutters clogged with leaves

are furiously swept.

The once beloved lounge,

recently demoted

to the veranda

tossed a further,

safe distance.


And finally all that is left is hope.

The following day, a lull. Radio stations repeated the same report. Fatigue set in and while the temptation to turn off communication of every sort was strong, the need to know of any change remained stronger.

### Such are the winds

It was three days

before the rhythm of hope,

chased by depression

became a pattern

with which to cope.

An evening
of community dining
of tales of disarray
of preparation
of play
and dismay
and resignation
stretched from water's edge to long table
to curbside.
As they lifted forks
cups and glasses,
to the northwest
rose premature darkness.

From the northeast a Herculean rumble
laboured into the black
upon which it's dousing load would tumble.
Looking to the sky relief encroached
on the faces of some
and others horror.

For a favourable wind for one
is a fearsome blow for others.

Then a further shift.
The makeshift settlement
came under threat
and the impulse to flee
shifted to one of siege.

*For if those that sort refuge moved further*
*they likely would be denied a return.*
*Leaving animals uncared for,*
*homes unprotected,*
*anxiety,*
*uncertainty increased.*
*Yet running short of supplies*
*and rations*
*the pull to relocate was strong.*
*But people such as these*
*are an independent and self-sufficient folk.*

*Shopping they did rarely,*
*preferring to harvest*
*the garden and river.*
*Convenience food came uneasily*
*to people*
*at home with dirt*
*under their nails*
*and blood on the boots.*

In all it was a week. Not quite long enough to really embed an idea of displacement but just long enough to mark a traumatic moment in the memory of most. People returned home in dribs and drabs. Those with livestock leading the way, for while the folk of the village had been keen to hastily trim their gardens of tinder and offer it as fodder, farmers large and small were eager not to stress their animals any further. So as the makeshift village of Shipwreck shore emerged it disappeared into the hills, the folk of the foreshore had their view back, and Robo, now trimmed and toothed, upon Kathy's return penned his last oration and left it unspoken.

### Return

*It was a week.*
*A week by the river*
*before they returned.*
*Trailing the ute*
*the old stock crate*
*clanked every pothole.*
*Goats swayed*
*unsure in their halters.*
*Past the abandoned orchard*
*limbs sagging*
*under crop*
*unthinned.*

*Past the old pickers' huts*
*paint peeling*
*roof lifting*
*chimney on the lean.*

*Over the bridge*
*and the rescue dog*
*doing circles in the front yard.*

*Neighbours pulling ribbons*
*of abandonment from front gates*
*and chickens*
*still playing dodge.*

They stopped
At the bottom of the drive.
Unsure of his traction
he slipped the ute
into low range.
Slowly they laboured
up the incline
to the sharp right hander before the level.
then rising again
before swinging around
a rough circle close to the paddock.
The goats were happy unshackled
and promptly
re-established
interactive order.

They rounded up the chooks.
Ducks like paparazzi followed
and soon the geese
honked their approach
as if a full bench in judgement.

The pigs seemed unperturbed
and even offered a curvaceous little bottle
booty from their archaeological efforts
as a welcome home present.

They left the ute loaded
not daring to settle.
Their valuables and nostalgia still packed away.

In the garden
lay many surprises.
Pumpkin stretching for the neighbours.
The first ripe tomatoes soft and spent,
bean pods about to crack.

He tipped away beer
brewed out filmy
thin and flat.
Pulled homemade sausages
and trapped wallaby quarters
from the sweaty freezer.
The cheeses
he'd been nurturing
slipped like ice cream
from overripe skins.

Together they lifted sodden rugs from the veranda
and stretched them over fences to dry.
They emptied bins and boats
and plastic drums of stale water
and scorched leaves
and watched across the valley
as neighbours tipped out pots and pans
set around the house
like enchanted magic circles.

They milked
as normal that afternoon,
though the air still thick
and beyond a vista
of young wattle
the next rise was black
and falling.

They dined as normal that afternoon,
though the chicken came plastic wrapped.

They dusted off the last bottle
of last year's homemade wine
and remembered how to laugh.
In the early evening
they picked blackberries
plump and ripe
that burst in their fingers
and stained their lips.

He pointed to ones they'd missed
dry and crumbly
or saggy and green with dusty mould.

She remarked,
"There'll be no jam this year."
And in the evening
and into the morning

*they watched*

*the hill with distrust*

*as smoke bled into the air*

*then lighted the nighttime sky.*

The folk of Hidden Valley remained on edge for many days as they set about rebuilding their farms and re-establishing their lifestyles. A collective sigh of relief was almost audible in the stillness of the first morning of an empty foreshore. The hills stood silent, scorched and just a little charred but full of folk thankful their homes remained. While a few outbuildings were lost and fence lines fallen, they came slowly to notice some places untouched, while next door a house and sheds poked out of a blackened landscape. A mosaic of smallholdings, small farms and what polite folk called lifestyle properties and mean folk called feral compounds, stood out against the charcoal scarred bush through which the fire had gorged itself.

As hotspots were watched over, contained and eventually forgotten, the wariness gave birth to the curious observation of the rush to normal, a return to what was and what was not. As what passed for normality in the Valley had been thrown into the air and folk had sung and danced together, shared their fears and hopes, drank and fallen over with strangers, discovered what really mattered and what really did not, began to fall back into old habits. It was the unknowing, the fear of silence, of space that spelt worry on faces. But just as people have done through history, most busied themselves resurrecting gardens, tidying around the house and leaving the bigger picture to fall as it fell, shaped by their combined way of simply getting on with it.

Robo returned to the furthermost reaches of the Valley, on the edge of the ashen West. Supplies came back over the Cold Shoulder, men went fishing in small boats again and yoga and piano classes resumed. There was soon an increase in visitor numbers, "fire tourist" or "ghouls" as the locals and blowins called them. It seemed that once again misfortune had smiled on Hidden Valley, gained it notoriety and sympathy from the greater populous, placed it on the map, like a forgotten place to be discovered.

Wreck House was booked out through the remainder of summer and into winter, bookings became essential at the Raft, especially on curry night, and the cafe reopened again but not as it had before. Having learned from the upheaval, it opened this time as a community enterprise run by folk from all over, putting on long table community dinners once a month that trailed down into the park and on a busy night along to Dinghy's, where memories of recent history and new projects could be shared.

As the Valley was shattered by fire from the west, so it coalesced in a manner unfamiliar, as predicted around a circle of displaced folk that sought refuge by the foreshore, by a young sociology student visiting her grandmother, who profoundly noted, over one of Reeves's burnt beef sausages, and mountain homebrew, as if straight from a text that "when a community is shattered it comes back together in a different form". She fell off her bucket shortly after, face down, but would return to carry out a protracted PhD study of the Valley, having convinced the university that Hidden Valley really was a community worthy of academic scrutiny.

Many of the valley folk did indeed seem to discover something new and different in themselves. Bob, of course had much work and shanghaied Shiv and Pete and JJ into helping out. JJ threw himself into the whole country homestead way of life. His man bun remained but his attire was less fussy, and he began to venture into remote parts of the valley, mostly in the company of Shiv and Pete and sometimes Kris and Chrissy. Gill took the occasional trip into the hills but was most intent on tracing and repairing the paths that seemed to thread cursively through the old garden.

＊

It was while out with Shiv and Pete, that JJ was led to the back of his land.

Just ten minutes walk from Pete's shack, through light bush that opened up to a crest, he gazed down at the house and out to the bay and the island beyond.

"It's beautiful," he gasped. "This is ours, wow, didn't realise it was so big."

"Certainly is. Starts at that big gumtree over there." Pete pointed at a massive tree, where the bush started to get thick. "Then it's mine and just down the hill is Flathead and after that Sitka and Sass, proper tree huggers those two. Graham and Sal are after that. Theirs is the big yellow gate, often got half a dozen kids' bikes in the drive."

They wandered back into the bush and in the direction of Flathead's, then on to the yellow gate, where, sure enough, a snaggle of bikes rested against the gate post. Walking back along the road Pete pointed out a few more entrances. "Lonely Ben is down there."

"Lonely?" queried JJ.

"Keeps himself to himself, not keen on visitors, harmless enough though."

"And this one?" JJ nodded at a rough driveway where the crude making of a track seemed to stop about six metres in.

"Vacant mate. Some mainlander bought it about ten years back. Came down once with his wife, camped overnight, saw a snake, got mud on their boots, heard a possum growl and never been down since."

"Happens a lot," Shiv added.

"No fire this way," JJ suddenly noted.

"Nothing to burn mate. Not much scrub. The people up here burn it quite often, usually in the winter. Just little bits. Flathead likes playing with fire.

He'll do your place for you if you want," said Shiv.

"What set fire to it?" questioned JJ, a bit concerned.

"Not like that. Not like what we just had, just keep the scrub down. It's traditional like. Mum and Dad get their place done."

JJ mused as they strolled and once back home related the idea to Gill, who'd rediscovered another path that twisted around a small grove of hazel nut trees.

❀

The drunken charcoal lipped prophecy had indeed come to be, JJ was on his way to bushman and farmer while Gill was beginning to work out that things could be grown without being in straight lines and uniform beds. It also coalesced in a much grander form too as a tribe of artisans, at one moment harmonising like smartly coordinated drones, and the next swinging from timbers as if an anarchic band of gibbons, teemed over a skeletal form that appeared to be growing out of the mud of the bay.

In wide hipped curves and elegant bows it rose. Ribs rough and bent seemed naturally twisted by western gales, yet unyielding in death as they were when rooted deep, heaved to life. Shortly planks were set in place, hewn from logs hauled down creeks, or salvaged, from ghost holed gums in mountain valleys.

The Young & Truthful, as she would be christened, stuck out from the Shipwreck mud. Two horns of an ancient beast, a craft drafted from the past, fitted out for the future, perhaps resting on the past but looking deep into the future. She would, one day, carry a cargo of gathered goods from Hidden Valley and the Siren Coast, propelled under sun and wind, to the gluttonous harbours of the north.

For now though, two dozen, or more, labourers and shipwrights, loped and strutted her growing bulk, pinning planks with copper spikes, tending steam rising from cauldrons and rusted, wire wrapped flues, set to flex all that entered. The vessel came to dwarf all else in bay, as too did the clatter and chatter of men and women with ancient tools and hope for tomorrow.

**The Beginning**

## About the Author

David L Hume has called Tasmania home for the past forty years. *Hidden Valley* is his first novella. He has two volumes of poetry to his name, *The Tale of Two Holes* and *The Tragedy of the Little Black House*. He has written for Ceramic Art and Perception and other arts journals and is the author of *Tourist Art and Souvenirs: The material Culture of Tourism*.

He lives off grid and mostly self-sufficiently at the end of a small valley near the Huon River.

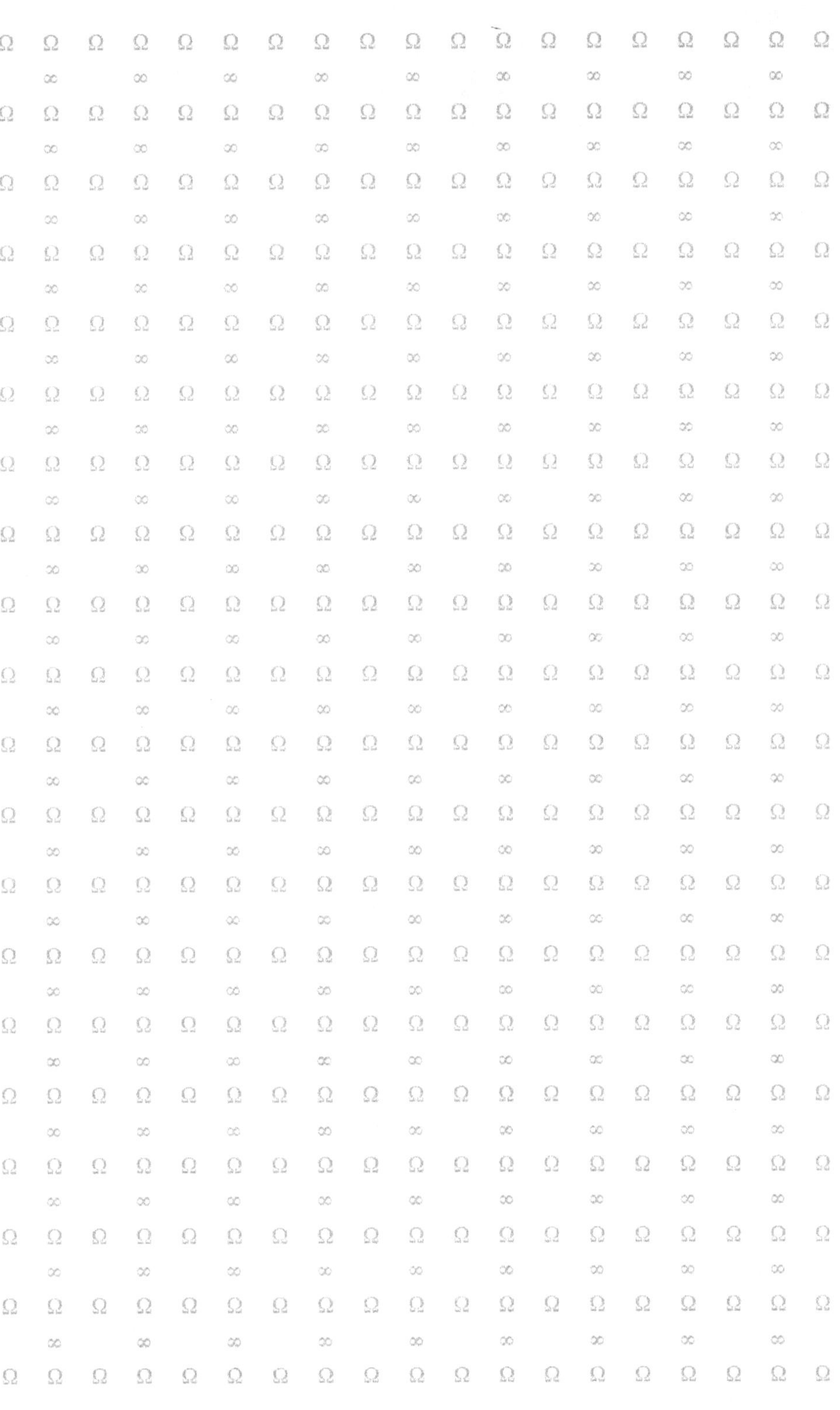

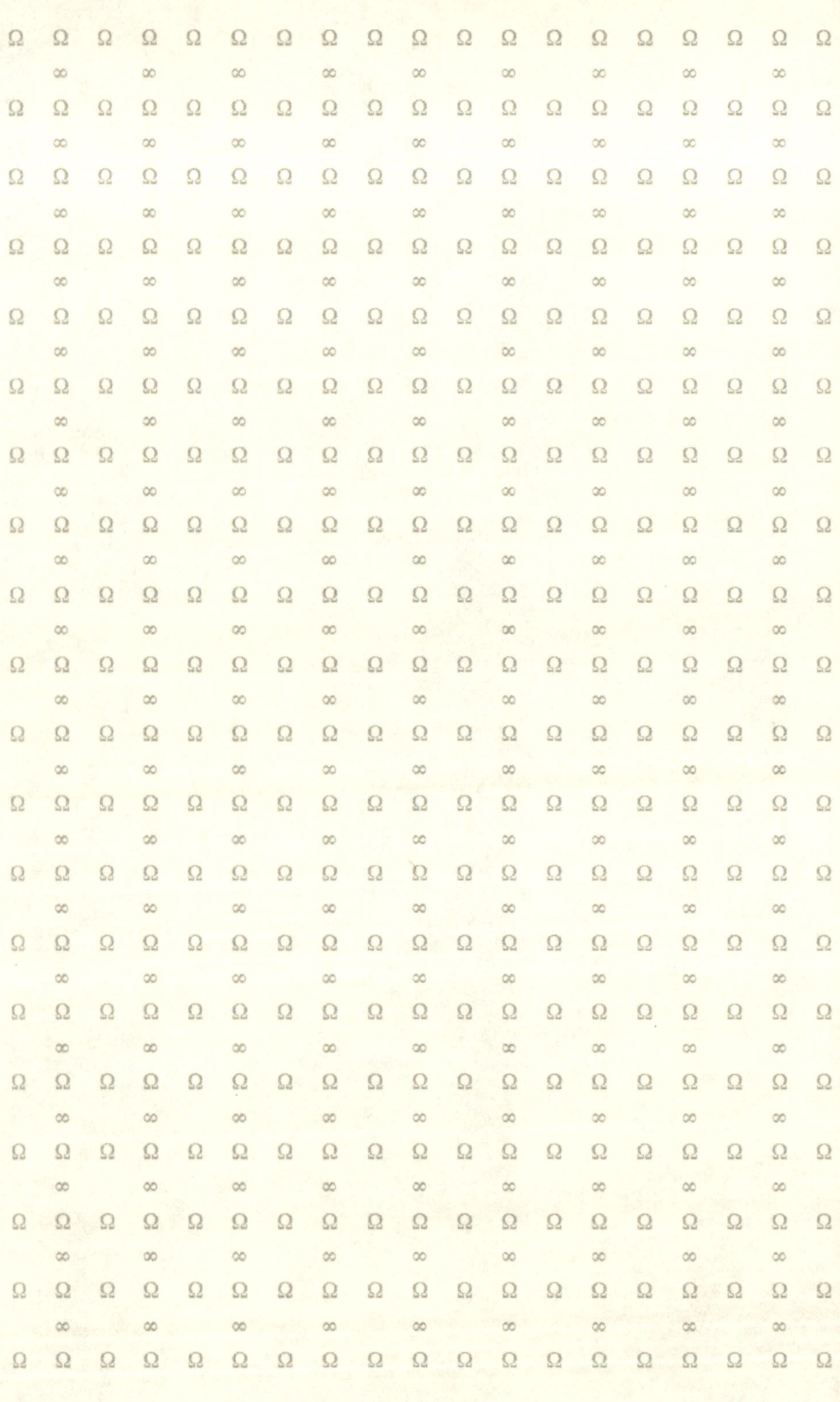

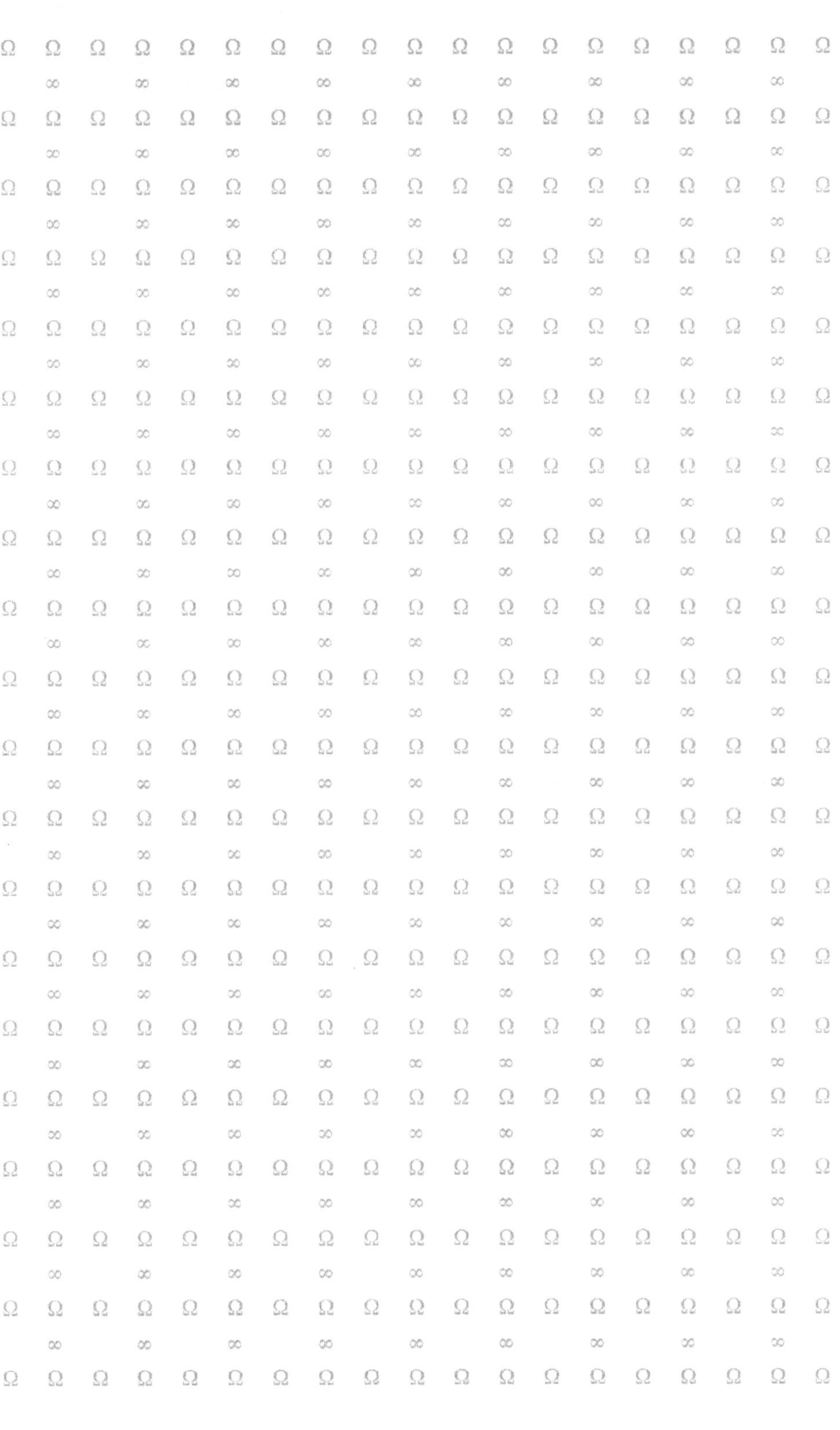

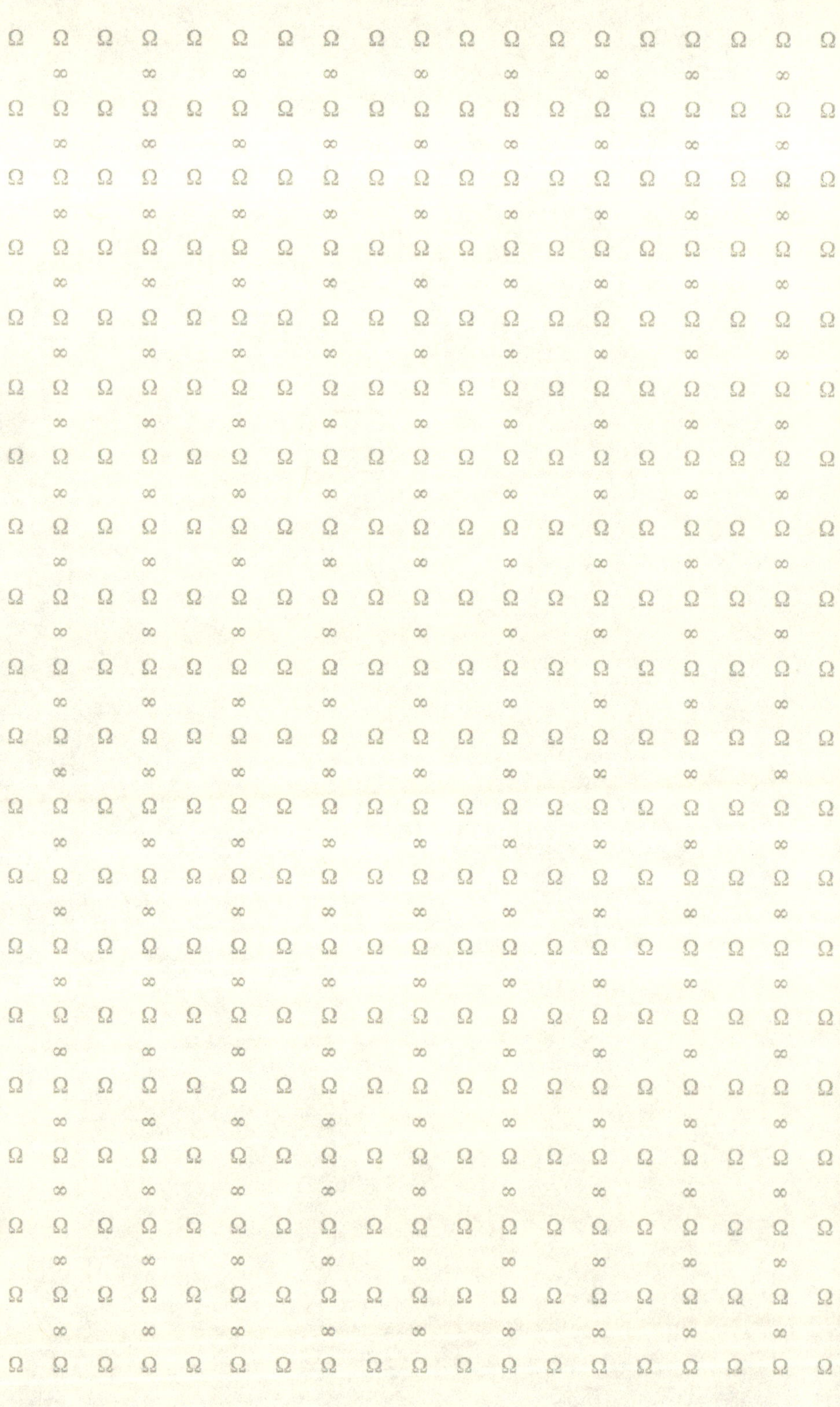